NEVER SAY GOOD-BYE

It's time for true confessions, Danielle.

"Tell us what happened last night!" Heather demanded.

Danielle's emerald eyes sparkled. "It's no big deal. Don and I just decided to skip the party."

"*What?*" the girls said in unison.

A mysterious, very satisfied smile settled on Danielle's face. *Score one for me.*

"Come on, Danielle," Teresa prodded. "We want details!"

"Lots of juicy, spicy details!" Heather agreed, more curious than ever.

"All you need to know is that—" Danielle hesitated. "Well, Don and I did set off some fireworks last night—even if no one else was there to witness the explosion!"

Merivale Mall

NEVER SAY GOOD-BYE

by Jana Ellis

Troll Associates

Library of Congress Cataloging-in-Publication Data

Ellis, Jana.
    Never say good-bye / by Jana Ellis
        p   cm.—(Merivale mall; #9)
    Summary Danielle and Don's romance peaks and turns rocky, while
Lori takes steps to help a homeless woman who wanders the mall
daily
    ISBN 0-8167-1618-8 (pbk.)
    [1 Shopping malls—Fiction] I Title   II Series. Ellis,
Jana.   Merivale mall; #9
PZ7 E472Nc 1990
[Fic]—dc20   89-34376

A TROLL BOOK, published by Troll Associates,
Mahwah, NJ 07430

Copyright © 1990 by Troll Associates, Mahwah, New Jersey

Printed in the United States of America.

10 9 8 7 6 5 4 3 2 1

NEVER SAY GOOD-BYE

CHAPTER ONE

"Tonight's the night!" Sixteen-year-old Danielle Sharp felt her blood race as she thought of the fabulous evening ahead.

"Boy, are you lucky. I've always thought that Don James was a major hunk," Teresa Woods claimed as she toyed with a bottle of nail polish.

"Definitely," Heather Barron called from a nearby cubicle where she was having her nails dipped and filed. "And now that he's Merivale's hometown hero, Don's the hottest guy around."

"And he's all mine!" Danielle beamed at her two best friends as she blew on her newly polished nails. Just months ago they had ribbed her for merely talking to Don James. But now that the tables had turned, Don was a wanted man—and Danielle was determined to snatch him up for herself.

"So what's the scoop for tonight? Is he picking you up on his motorcycle?" Teresa asked, wrinkling her freckled nose.

"You're just jealous," Danielle said, lowering her voice so that other customers in the exclusive salon couldn't listen in. Her emerald eyes narrowed in a cutting glare. "I didn't hear you raving about *your* date for the party!"

When her friend didn't answer, Danielle cast a satisfied glance at her glossy nails and stepped away from the manicurist's table. Teresa had a lot of nerve making snide remarks about Don. Especially when she didn't have any guys breaking down *her* front door!

Now that her hair and nails were absolutely flawless, Danielle was beginning to get excited about tonight's party at Ashley Shepard's house. All the popular teenagers from Atwood Academy would be there. The black-tie bash was the number-one social event of the season, and Danielle was going to walk in on the arm of Merivale's most gorgeous prospect—Don James.

"You're next for a manicure, Miss Woods," said the attendant.

To the Manor Born was bustling with brisk attendants in crisp smocks and chattering women of all ages. The girls had come to the posh salon in Merivale Mall to be primped and prepped for tonight's big event.

Teresa plopped into the chair, still examining the array of nail polish displayed on an engraved gold tray. "I'm torn between Very Berry and Mauve Magic."

"What color is your dress?" Heather asked from the other side of the screen.

"Dusty rose—and outrageous!"

"Try Five Alarm Fire," Danielle suggested. She was glad she'd chosen Really Ruby for her nails. The glossy red shade would look great with her slinky black outfit.

"Does Ashley know you're bringing Merivale's man of the year to her party?" Heather asked.

A surge of excitement swept through Danielle as she thought about her public debut with Don. "Ashley nearly choked when I told her. But she was thrilled. From what I hear, even her *parents* want to meet him."

"Well, he's still quite a celebrity after that incredible rescue." With a dreamy look Heather tipped her head to the side, her straight black hair gleaming in the beam of one of the salon's track lights. "The way he saved that little kid—"

"Lilac Lunacy," Teresa interrupted. "Or maybe Perfectly Peachy."

"Teresa! Make up your mind!" Heather called. "Anyway, Don was brave and courageous and all that. But the fact that he's adorable has made him a super hero."

Nibbling at the inside of her lip, Danielle considered her friend's words. Although she'd always had a thing for sexy, dark-eyed Don James, Danielle had tried to hide her feelings.

Seventeen-year-old Don James was rough around the edges. He lived in a run-down farmhouse on the outskirts of town with a pack of older guys who were definitely not dating material. Wild, rowdy guys who wore black leather jackets and drove souped-up motorcycles—guys who would curl the toes of any socially acceptable girl in Merivale.

As far as Danielle and her friends were concerned, Don had been off limits—until recently. When a toddler slipped through a railing at Merivale Mall, Don thought fast and caught the boy in his arms. His quick thinking and courage had saved the kid's life.

And suddenly Merivale's black sheep was on the top of everyone's date list.

You used to tease me whenever I got within twenty feet of the guy, Danielle thought as she listened to her friends bicker about who would drive to the party.

And now they were jealous! Well, it served them right. Teresa and Heather were her best friends, but they were also total snobs. They wouldn't admit to liking a boy unless absolutely everyone approved of him.

"Did you ever try Pink Persuasion?" Teresa's voice brought Danielle back to earth.

"Never. I detest pink." Danielle slung her buttery leather bag over her shoulder and checked her slender gold watch. Three-thirty!

Since so many women came to the salon to get spruced up for Saturday night, they were running late. "Looks like you two are going to be a while, and I still have a few things to pick up in the mall. See you at the party?"

"In living color," Heather answered in her whispery voice.

"Eight o'clock," Teresa reminded her.

Danielle nodded. "Don's picking me up at seven-thirty so we can spend some time together before things begin to roll."

Teresa's brown eyes widened with envy. "Some girls have all the luck!"

"Luck?" Already on her way out the door, Danielle spun around, her hair whipping over her shoulder like a curtain of copper. "Not luck. It's charisma!"

"That's it!" Teresa squealed, plucking a tiny bottle from the display of polish. "The perfect color for me—Coral Charisma!"

From her spot behind the counter at Tio's Tacos, Lori Randall waved at her cousin. Danielle's greeting was hurried as she rushed along the first floor of Merivale Mall.

"That's some outfit," said Isabel Vasquez,

the cook at Tio's. She stood beside Lori and stared at Danielle, who ducked into Platterpus, a popular record store. "I wonder how many cows lost their hides for those jeans," Isabel added as she picked up a huge can of stewed tomatoes.

Decked out in ginger-colored suede slacks and a chocolate-brown sweater, Danielle was a knockout. "She always looks great," Lori said.

Although they were cousins, Lori and Danielle traveled in different circles. Three years ago Danielle's father, Mike Sharp, had struck it rich with the development of his prized real estate project, Merivale Mall. Ever since then Danielle had attended a different school, hung out with different friends—even shopped in different stores.

Lori didn't begrudge her cousin the neat things in her life, but sometimes she missed the easy friendship they used to have.

After Danielle's stunning outfit, Lori's work uniform was a dreadful sight. She looked down with a frown. The fluorescent yellow apron now bore a red salsa stain from a messy enchilada. The lunch rush had been especially busy. In an effort to keep the line moving, Lori hadn't even taken her usual break.

The door to the back office swung open and the manager emerged, whistling a cheerful tune. "Good news, Ernie?" Lori asked her boss.

"A good day," he answered with a smile.

"With a few more lunchtime crowds like that, I'll be whistling *and* singing."

"Heaven help us," Isabel said wryly, and both girls laughed.

Ernie Goldbloom playfully wagged a finger at them, then paused, as if noticing Lori for the first time. "Now, wait a minute," he said. "What are you doing here? Isn't this your usual break time?"

"Lori likes my cooking so much, she's decided she'll never leave," Isabel teased.

Lori shrugged as Ernie looked on disapprovingly. "The lines were so long, I really couldn't get away," she explained.

"Out you go!" Ernie ordered. "I like my employees to enjoy their work, but this is ridiculous! Now, scram!"

"Consider me history." Lori pulled off the hideous apron and tossed it under the counter. "I'll be back in fifteen minutes."

"Make that thirty," Ernie said. "This place will be dead until suppertime."

Lori slipped out of the Mexican fast-food place and into the sunny, open space of Merivale Mall. It felt good to remove the hair net and shake out her silky blond hair.

With a twinge of longing she glanced at the illuminated sign for Hobart Electronics. She frequently spent her breaks with her boyfriend, Nick Hobart, whose father owned the shop.

But today Nick was working at his father's warehouse, preparing for inventory.

Despite the animated crowds of shoppers, the mall seemed like an empty playground today. Lori's friend Patsy Donovan had the day off, so there was no use going over to the Cookie Connection to visit her either.

But she still had Merivale Mall at her fingertips. And she couldn't let her break go to waste just because her friends were busy elsewhere!

Walking past one of the mall's bubbling fountains, Lori stepped onto a sleek chrome escalator. Might as well check out the hot new fashions in the boutiques on the upper level.

As the escalator swept past the second level, Lori noticed a tiny, feeble woman with a purple beret perched on a stone bench. Lori smiled at the woman, but Nora Pringle didn't acknowledge her. She merely muttered something to herself and kept scribbling on a pad of paper.

Nora Pringle spent most of her days sitting on a sunny bench at Merivale Mall. Lori was used to seeing the forlorn lady dressed in layers of tattered clothing. Deep in her heart Lori was pleased that Merivale Mall provided a clean, warm refuge for a lonely old woman like Nora.

The escalator climbed on, taking Lori to the very top. The decorative windows on the fourth level were a fashion-lover's feast! Although Lori couldn't afford to buy anything in the exclusive designer shops at Merivale Mall, she loved to browse. Buttons and bangles, fringes and bows—they were all inspiration for Lori's plans.

Her ultimate dream was to become a famous fashion designer, and Lori worked hard to make it all come true. She was always whipping up stunning creations on her sewing machine, making a few dollars go a long way when it came time for a prom dress or a Halloween costume.

A patterned knit minidress in the window of Facades caught her eye. Lori was intrigued by the way the jagged blue lightning-bolt pattern was embroidered on the material, giving the design texture and dimension. She made a mental note of the technique, then strolled on to the next shop window.

By the time Lori reached the end of the mall, she'd discovered a few techniques that would be useful on her own creations.

As it was still too early to head back to Tio's, she decided to sneak off to her own little refuge, the loading docks of Merivale Mall, and rest her tired feet for a while.

The elevator at the end of the mall took her directly to the lowest level. Although the stores above were bustling with shoppers, it was relatively quiet down here. Most of the deliveries were handled in the early morning and afternoon.

This was her special place. She often came

here to think, to clear her head, to get away from the hustle and bustle of the mall.

Lori plopped down on a wooden crate marked ATHLETE'S ARCH: FOOTBALLS. It made her think of Nick, who was the star quarterback of the Atwood Academy football team.

She pulled her knees up under her chin and smiled. She was so used to having Nick around—handsome, wonderful Nick. At this point her life would seem so empty without him. Here he was, spending just one day working in his father's warehouse, and she couldn't stop thinking about him!

Just then the door to the stairwell flew open, startling Lori. In a flurry of paper shopping bags and raggedy scarves, Nora Pringle scuttled onto the loading platform just a few yards away from Lori. The poor woman was obviously out of breath, yet she hurriedly stumbled forward.

"Are you okay?" Lori asked, leaping to her feet.

The old woman had lost her purple hat, and her wiry silver hair stuck out at odd angles. Nora Pringle paused and narrowed her eyes suspiciously, as if she didn't trust even Lori. Then a loud noise in the stairwell sent her scurrying on.

The stairwell door was flung open again, banging loudly against the brick wall. Three boys emerged, giggling and waving Nora's purple beret in their hands!

"Hey, lady," the freckle-faced boy shouted. "You forgot your hat!"

The other two boys cackled and howled as if this were the funniest thing they'd ever heard.

Lori recognized the kids as students from Merivale Junior High. "What are you doing?" she demanded.

The boys paused in their pursuit of Nora to check out Lori, a slim wisp of a golden-haired teenager.

After a shrewd appraisal, the freckled boy, obviously the leader, shrugged and tossed Nora's hat to the ground. "Come on, you guys," he called to his friends. "Let's get out of here!"

CHAPTER TWO

"I'm sorry, miss, but I'm afraid I just sold our last copy."

"That's impossible." Danielle cocked her head so that the bangs of her fiery red hair teased at the corner of one eye. "You must have one more copy of the Bad Boys' recording *somewhere*," she told the clerk, flashing him a smile to melt his heart. "For *me*? I don't care whether it's a record, tape, or CD. I've just got to have *Stardust Dreams*!"

The salesclerk shook his head. "I've already checked the storeroom. That recording is such a smash hit, we haven't been able to keep up with the demand." He shrugged. "Why don't you try again next week?"

Because I need it tonight! Danielle's eyes became molten green fire as her temper flared. That record was an important part of her plan for this evening. But she wasn't about to explain herself to a lame-brained clerk at Platterpus.

"Next week is too late," she snapped before striding away from the counter. How could they be so dumb? She was ready to lay down top dollar for a record album, and they couldn't even keep it in stock!

Still fuming, she checked the bins again, but there were no copies of *Stardust Dreams* anywhere. Then she noticed a toddler playing at the front of the store. The little girl was leaning toward the display case, pointing at the flashing bulbs and saying, "Light!"

At that moment a bulb flashed in Danielle's brain. The display case! Platterpus had to have a copy of *Stardust Dreams* in the window!

She rushed over to the edge of the display case and stood behind the little girl. The back of the store window was closed off, but there was room to peek in at the edge. The window was aglow with splashy posters and flashing lights. And there at the edge were two copies of the Bad Boys' album and one of the CD!

"Finally!" Danielle said, nudging the toddler aside so she could reach into the display case.

"Lights!" the little girl repeated, her lower lip protruding in a pout.

Danielle had to lean so far forward, she almost fell into the display area. But at last, her smooth, freshly manicured fingers closed over the two album covers.

"Gotcha!" she said, holding them up for a closer look. She frowned. Something wasn't right here. They were too light. The blue and silver foil album covers were empty!

"I can't believe this!" Danielle flung the empty record jackets to the floor and lunged into the display case once again.

This time her efforts were rewarded. The CD package was still factory-sealed—with the compact disc of the hottest, most romantic hit song inside!

"Excuse me, miss—" The salesclerk looked irritated.

"I'll take this." Danielle handed him the CD and dug into her purse for her wallet.

The clerk frowned. "We're not allowed to dismantle the window display."

"Don't be ridiculous," Danielle insisted, fixing him with a haughty glare. "You shouldn't be advertising a record you don't have. Now, will you ring up this sale—or do I have to report you to your manager?"

After a moment's hesitation the clerk gave in. Danielle smiled as he handed her the receipt. Now that she'd finagled a copy of *Stardust Dreams*, the perfect evening could begin.

As Danielle was a total perfectionist, she

had planned this night from start to finish. She'd gotten head-to-toe treatment at To the Manor Born, she'd bought a knockout dress, and now she had found sweeping, powerful music to complete the effect when Don arrived at her house.

One look at Danielle, and Don James would be a goner.

And by the time the band played its last song, Don would be staring into her emerald eyes—endlessly, hopelessly in love with her!

Nora's eyes shone with fear as she cowered in a corner of the loading dock area. Her body was wedged behind a wall of cardboard boxes, but she peered out at the boys with the frozen expression of a hunted animal.

The mere sight of the frightened woman wrenched at Lori's heart.

Well, at least the bullies had backed off. The harsh laughter of the fleeing boys echoed down the stairwell, sending a chill down Lori's spine. She couldn't believe the ugly scene she'd just witnessed. How could those kids be so cruel?

As Lori turned away from the exit, she considered the sort of life Nora Pringle led. Moving from one bench to another, eating discarded food from garbage cans, gathering comfort only from her collection of bulging shopping bags and her scribbled notes, which were just gibberish to the rest of the world.

Lori wanted to cry at the injustice of the whole situation. Nora Pringle had so little . . . and Lori had so much.

The contrast was so stark, it made her wince. Lori Randall was blessed with a cozy home, a loving family, dynamite friends, a neat car, and Nick, the most wonderful guy in the world.

As Lori walked across the loading docks, she made herself a solemn promise. Somehow, she was going to do something special for Nora Pringle. Surely there was something she could do to help the desolate woman!

Maybe she could help Nora get a job? Or perhaps Lori could even find a home for her.

"Miss Pringle," she called, gingerly approaching the stack of boxes. She didn't want to scare the poor woman again after the fright she'd just suffered.

"Miss Pringle," Lori repeated.

The corner was dark and eerie. Lori took a deep breath before peeking around the wall of cardboard boxes.

But the corner was empty.

"Miss Pringle," Lori called again as she searched nearby doorways and cubbyholes.

But no one answered. Lori's voice was the only sound in the silence of the abandoned delivery area.

Nora Pringle was gone.

"Every time I see your face . . . stardust dreams . . ."

The melodic ballad wafted through the Sharp mansion, filling Danielle's suite of rooms with wailing guitar riffs and jazz piano. Danielle felt transported by the music as she finished dressing for her date.

The song reminded her of the romantic soundtracks used in old movies, like the moody background stuff they'd play while the camera zoomed in on Greta Garbo's face, the focus softening as tears began to slide down her cheeks.

Danielle adored Garbo. There was something so elegant and mysterious about the actress . . . something that made men melt at her feet.

I guess Greta and I have a lot in common, Danielle thought as she practiced a mysterious smile in the mirror. She picked up a bottle of her favorite perfume—Fallen Angel—and sprayed a cloud of scent behind each ear.

Don would flip when he saw this dress. She looked just like Greta Garbo in *Mata Hari*.

Danielle stepped closer to the full-length mirror to get a better look at herself. Her strapless black gown positively sizzled. And with her sequined silk-chiffon jacket and diamond drop earrings, she would light up the night.

When she and Don walked into Ashley Shepard's house, eyes would pop. And everyone would agree that they were the hottest couple to hit Merivale in centuries!

"Every time I hear your voice . . . stardust dreams . . ."

Since her parents had already left for the Millers' bridge party, Danielle had the compact disc player in the den cranked all the way up.

They don't even care enough to stick around and see me out the door. The thought hurt Danielle more than she wanted to admit. Serena and Mike Sharp were so caught up in their own business and social events, they could never seem to find time for their youngest daughter.

Frowning, Danielle sat down at her lacquered vanity table, leaned toward the mirror, and added another layer of green sparkle to her eyelids.

Maybe she was better off with her parents out of the way tonight. Her mother would probably find something wrong with Danielle's appearance, while her father would just hem and haw and try to look interested, even though his mind was occupied elsewhere.

"And when you hold me close . . . stardust dreams . . ."

But nothing was going to spoil this magical evening. If her parents were unhappy, that was their problem. Danielle had a date with a special guy, and she was determined to have a blast.

With her make-up complete, she leaned back for a shrewd assessment.

"Gorgeous!"

Her artfully tossed hair was perfection it-
self, a long, shiny halo of copper fire. She glanced
at her diamond-studded watch. She was running a little late, but that was okay. Only fools
and wallflowers arrived at a party on time. But
it was already after eight, and Don should have
been here ages earlier.

I guess boys need time to primp, too, Danielle
thought as she went downstairs to replay *Stardust Dreams* one more time.

After she'd reset the disc player, Danielle
went to one of the floor-to-ceiling windows near
the front vestibule and peeked outside.

The night was dark, with only a sliver of
moonlight dancing along the tiny leaves of the
well-trimmed hedges. There were no headlights
in the circular driveway. No rumble of a car
engine.

Where was Don?

Fighting off a twinge of annoyance, she
sighed and went back upstairs to apply some
finishing touches.

"Like a vision in the dark . . . stardust dreams . . ."

But when Danielle looked in the mirror once
again, she folded her arms and shrugged. She
looked smashing! "Why tamper with perfection?" she said aloud as she found a comfortable spot on the white leather sofa in her
bedroom alcove.

Waiting for Don was getting nerve-racking—
especially since patience had never been one of

Danielle's strongest qualities. Ten minutes later, still tapping her nails against the leather arm of the sofa, Danielle frowned.

Where was he?

Could he have forgotten?

She'd just begun to pace when she heard the familiar chime of the doorbell. At last!

Danielle checked her watch as she raced down the stairs. They were really late now, but in the long run it wouldn't matter. They could still make a major splash at the party.

At the foot of the stairs she paused and took a deep breath, wanting to appear cool and casual. It wouldn't be too savvy to let Don see her breathless with excitement. Then she opened the front door—and all her composure fizzled in a split second.

Don James stood in the doorway looking dark and gritty in faded jeans and a beat-up black leather jacket!

CHAPTER THREE

"Hey, Red." Don's smile had a harsh edge to it.

"Don . . ." Danielle's mouth dropped open as she stared at him.

Had Don gone nuts? He couldn't possibly go to Ashley Shepard's black-tie party dressed that way! He even had black grease stains under his fingernails!

Don leaned against the doorjamb as if he'd been hanging there all night. "You going to let me in, Red?" he asked. "Or are you just going to nail me with that nasty look?"

"You can come in," she said. "But I can't believe you have the nerve to show up dressed like a grease monkey!" She flung the door wide and marched into the living room.

How could he do this to her? There was no way she was going to Ashley's party with a slob, so the whole night was as good as ruined. Thanks to Don and his late, scraggly appearance!

In the living room she dropped into an overstuffed chair. Time for a good sulk while Don stewed in his own guilt.

When he followed her into the room a moment later, Danielle was determined to give him the cold shoulder. But she changed her mind when she noticed the downcast look in his dark, glimmering eyes.

Don was crouched on the armrest of the sofa, as if he were too riled up to sit down. He seemed completely lost in thought.

"What's wrong?" Danielle asked. She was still mad about the party, but Don's dark mood intrigued her.

It must be something horrible for him to have disappointed me like this. Danielle looked down at her nails. "We were *supposed* to go to Ashley's party tonight."

Still staring off into the distance, Don nodded. "I know. Sorry, Red."

Although his words were sincere, Danielle could tell that the party was the last thing on his mind. She shifted around to get a better look at him. This problem had to be a whopper!

"So what happened?" she prodded him.

"I got the shaft today." A shadow of gloom crossed Don's face. "My brother handed me my walking papers. He's going off to school, so he can't be my guardian angel anymore."

That didn't sound so bad to Danielle. She'd never liked the idea of Don living with his older brother and those rowdy bikers. And that ramshackle house on the edge of town was the pits. Don had always seemed comfortable with the situation, since he didn't get along with his parents, but Danielle wasn't crazy about his motley crew of housemates.

Exciting possibilities flitted through Danielle's mind. Don could get his own apartment, a nice place near the center of town. She could even help him decorate it. "So then you're on your own now. It won't be that bad."

Don shook his head. "Between my part-time job at the garage and one more year at Merivale High, I could never afford my own place. And I'm only seventeen. My parents want me to move back with them—pronto."

His parents! Danielle had nearly forgotten about them.

"I don't know why they want me so bad all of a sudden. They've always hated me. And they do their best to make my life miserable."

Now Danielle understood Don's depression. Although she'd never met Mr. and Mrs. James, Don had told her about some of their spiteful antics.

What a crummy deal! Since Danielle knew how it felt to live in a war zone, her heart went out to Don.

"What about your brother?" she asked. "Aren't you mad at him for leaving you in the lurch?"

Don stood up and went to stare out the huge window. "I can't blame him. This is a new start for him—going off to cooking school and trying to do something with his life. He's always wanted to be a chef. He's a wild man on a griddle, so I think he'll do well. I hope everything works out for him."

Silhouetted against the dark glass, Don's muscular six foot two frame seemed so strong and powerful. It was hard to believe he was powerless in the face of these circumstances.

It was hard to believe that his whole world was falling apart.

Danielle glanced down at the sizzling outfit she'd so artfully assembled. Oddly enough, she no longer cared about Ashley's stupid party. Don was really depressed. And right now it was more important just to be with him—even if it meant missing the number-one social event of the season.

For her the party was over. She slipped off her sequined jacket and snakeskin high heels and carelessly tossed them onto the carpet. Then she tiptoed over to where Don stood, staring out the window.

What could she say? She wasn't too good at dealing with problems. In the Sharp family, problems were always swept under the carpet and ignored. Such nuisances weren't supposed to exist in the perfect home.

And even Danielle's friends were immune to problems. In the years that she'd been best friends with Teresa and Heather, the three girls had never banded together in a crisis. Members of the most exclusive clique at Atwood Academy always pretended that their lives were worry-free. One little problem could send any popular girl plummeting to the dregs of Atwood's in crowd.

Danielle's heart pounded as she stood behind Don, wanting to reach out and help him. But for the first time in her life she was at a loss for words.

"I—I wish there were something I could say . . . something I could do . . ."

She paused when she sensed his tension. The truth was, there was nothing she could do to help Don at this moment. If his parents wanted him under their roof—and under their thumb—that was where he'd live. At least for the next year or so.

"I'm really sorry," Danielle said.

"It's okay." Don turned around to face her.

The intense look in his dark eyes almost took Danielle's breath away. Those eyes penetrated her heart, searching deep inside her but still accepting everything they saw.

They'd been through a lot together. And Don probably knew Danielle better than anyone else in the world. He knew the *real* Danielle —the one with feelings and fears—and he was still crazy about her.

He slipped his arms around her waist. "You know, just talking to you about this stuff makes me feel better. You're a pretty good listener, Red. And besides, you look great." He held her away from him, lifting her hand and leading her in a spin, as if they were dancing.

With polished grace Danielle twirled around, then held out her arms like a fashion model. Her dazzling performance made Don crack a smile.

"And I had to go and mess everything up." He shrugged. "This afternoon, when my brother came to the garage to break the news, I was kind of stunned. I kept going through the motions, but all I could think was—it's over. No more freedom."

Danielle frowned. Life with Don's parents sounded like a prison sentence.

"By the time I was finished at work, my mind was scattered all over the place—frazzled. I jumped on my bike and hit the road. Went cruising through the mountains. Tried to think of a way out of this mess. Before I knew it, the sun had set—and I had a feeling it was late. I drove straight over here." He held up his hands. "Didn't even get a chance to scrub off the grease from the engine I overhauled."

One corner of Danielle's evenly glossed lips

lifted in a teasing grin. "That's one problem I can solve. We have plenty of soap and water."

"And I meant what I said about the party. I know that stuff's important to you," he said sincerely. "Sorry, Red."

She waved off his apology with a neatly manicured hand. "It probably would have been a snooze anyway. If you've been to one black-tie affair, you might as well have been to a million."

"Is that right?" Don's smile was skeptical. "Well, anyway, it's a shame to waste a whole Saturday night with such a gorgeous girl."

"And why should it go to waste?" Danielle asked, whipping a tousled strand of copper hair over her shoulder.

Don laughed. "All right, Red. What wicked plans are you brewing in that devious mind of yours?"

"Nothing too decadent. I just thought that since we have the place to ourselves, we might as well hang around and watch a movie."

"Saturday night at the Sharp mansion?" Don teased. "What's not to like?"

"And if you're nice to me, I'll even see if I can rustle up something to eat."

Don gave her a wry look. "Come on, Red. You're talking to the guy who's been after you since the sixth grade. I'm *always* nice to you."

While Don checked out the Sharps' collection of videos in the den, Danielle sauntered into the kitchen.

When Danielle's father had designed and built this house, he'd filled the kitchen with the sleekest, most modern appliances on the market. They were all quite impressive, but the only thing the family really used was the oversized refrigerator, large enough to store the bulky trays from Premier Caterers. Although Serena Sharp liked people to think she was a gourmet cook, the truth was she had trouble boiling water.

"Let's see . . ." She opened the refrigerator and leaned against the enormous door. Wrinkling her nose at a tray of soggy hors d'oeuvres left over from her mother's recent cocktail party, Danielle grabbed a platter of cheeses and a bag of microwave popcorn.

By the time she returned to the den, Don was stretched out on the sofa with a movie cued up in the VCR. His jacket had been flung across an empty chair and, from the clean scent in the air, Danielle could tell that he'd just washed up.

"Not bad for a helpless debutante," Don said when he noticed the tray of sodas and snacks.

"And you thought I couldn't cook," Danielle said, handing him the bowl of popcorn.

The movie he'd chosen was an old Greta Garbo film, one of Danielle's favorites. As she sat on the sofa next to him, Danielle was surprised at the way this evening had turned out.

This was ten times more romantic than dancing and sipping punch at a kiddie party. And maybe, just maybe, she and Don had made their mark on Merivale after all. Danielle knew one thing for sure: Their no-show performance tonight would start tongues wagging tomorrow.

Lost in the sultry image of Garbo on the screen, she leaned back on the cushy black leather sofa. Don's hand had been resting behind her, and now he moved it just an inch so that it brushed at a wisp of fiery red hair on her shoulder.

His touch sent a tingle down Danielle's spine. A moment later he swept her hair back and cupped her smooth, bare shoulder. His hand was callused, but it was also warm and gentle.

When Danielle turned to look in his eyes, his face was so close she could feel his breath against her cheek. Her heart seemed to be pounding in double time, and she wondered if he could hear it.

She wanted to ask him more about his plans, but her mind became a jumble of thoughts when Don squeezed her shoulder.

Oh my gosh! He's going to kiss me!

As Danielle closed her eyes, Don gave her a gentle kiss, sending shivers from her head straight down to her toes.

"Every time I see your face . . . stardust dreams . . ."

Danielle let the Bad Boys' recording play one last time as she slipped between the crisp sheets of her bed. She and Don had gotten so engrossed in the movie, she'd never had a chance to play it for him.

But with or without *Stardust Dreams*, Danielle Sharp would never forget the most romantic evening of her life.

Collapsing against a wall of lacy pillows, Danielle remembered the way she'd felt in Don's arms. And his fabulous, earth-shattering kisses . . .

Oh, she'd been kissed before. But tonight was completely, absolutely, positively different.

Because she'd been kissed by Don James.

They'd spent the rest of the evening talking and kidding around. At one point Danielle had been tempted to tell him about her parents' troubles. Very few people knew about Mike and Serena Sharp's constant bickering. The couple tried to present a pleasant façade to the world, and Danielle had always been too embarrassed to reveal the truth to anyone—except Don. There was something special about his easy, laid-back smile—something that encouraged Danielle to share her troubles with him.

And now Don had confided in her. Danielle was elated. Never before had she felt so close to a guy. Maybe the hot romance she'd bragged about was really coming true!

There was just one tiny flaw in the picture. Things were great now, but what about after Don moved back home?

In a few days he'd be living under his parents' thumb again. And there was bound to be an explosion. Would Don's problems at home take a toll on their romance? She knew from experience that when your house is a war zone, it's hard to think about anything—or anyone else.

Danielle rolled over and punched at the pillow beneath her. Her heart ached for Don when she thought of the misery his parents were sure to cause him. And she'd die if Mr. and Mrs. James tore him away from her.

She gave the pillow another punch before she reached over to turn off the light. "Family feuds are the worst," she whispered amid the darkness of her room.

CHAPTER FOUR

"One, two, three, kick! Back, two, three, kick!" Ann Larson called out encouragingly as she led the class through the aerobics lesson.

Dressed in a sexy silver leotard with black tights, Danielle stole into the back of the richly carpeted exercise room of The Body Shoppe, an exclusive fitness club located on the third level of Merivale Mall.

Although Danielle tried to slip into the back row of girls without causing a stir, her two best friends never missed a trick.

With a toss of her long brown bangs, Teresa turned her head to scrutinize the latecomer. When she saw that it was Danielle, she did a double-take and nudged Heather.

Heather's ice-blue gaze sliced through Danielle with more than a hint of suspicion.

What is this, an inquisition? Danielle gritted her teeth as she reached for the ceiling and stretched from the waist. So she'd missed the first half of the class. Big deal! When she'd agreed to meet her friends for a Sunday morning workout, she hadn't planned on staying up late to spend the previous night nestled in Don James's arms!

On the other hand, she had intended this meeting to be a sort of victory celebration. Confident that she and Don would make a splash at Ashley's party, she'd wanted a chance to gloat afterward.

But now Heather and Teresa were sending her glares as sharp as needles, ready to burst her bubble.

No way! Danielle rushed through the cool-down exercises, charged with a new challenge.

"That's it for today," Ann announced. "You all did great."

Although Danielle and her friends enjoyed Ann's aerobics class, they didn't socialize with the tall, chestnut-haired part-time instructor. A student at Merivale High, Ann was a good friend of Lori Randall's. *One of the peasants*, Danielle thought. Despite the fact that Lori was a sweet kid, Danielle never ceased to be embarrassed by her unsophisticated cousin, as wholesome as apple pie and perky as summer sunshine. How boring!

"If it isn't Cinderella!" Teresa tossed Danielle a towel. "What happened? Did your pumpkin forget how to turn into a coach?"

"Having dating troubles, Danielle?" Heather pulled off a braided headband and shook out her glossy black hair. "Did dear old Don stand you up? Or are you just afraid to let him out after dark?"

Danielle seethed as her friends' snide remarks gave way to malicious laughter. How dare they!

Slinging the towel around her neck, Danielle looked each girl squarely in the eye. "Sorry to disappoint you, kids. But Don and I decided to skip the milk and cookies at Ashley-washley's house. We had more important things on our minds. And we find pin the tail on the donkey a tad childish. Don't you agree?"

Before they could answer, Danielle spun on her heel and strode into the locker room. She needed a dip in the Jacuzzi to calm her down. She needed time to think. She needed to come up with a whopping story, because there was no way she could tell the Atwood snobs about Don's problem. They would howl in the face of his anguish!

In the meantime, maybe Heather and Teresa would spend some time in the sauna—shrinking their egos down to size!

Five minutes later the girls caught up with her. Lulled by the effervescent sounds of the bubbling water, Danielle had just closed her eyes when she heard two bodies slip into the whirlpool.

"Okay, Danielle. It's time for true confessions. Tell us what happened last night!" Heather demanded.

Danielle's eyes opened to emerald slits. "It's no big deal. Don and I just decided to skip the party."

"What?" the girls demanded in unison.

A mysterious, very satisfied smile settled on Danielle's face. *Score one for me.*

"Ashley is really insulted, since you didn't call or anything," Teresa added.

"She'll get over it." Danielle sighed and slid down in the pool so that the soothing water covered her smooth shoulders.

The other girls' eyes widened in amazement.

"You've got to be kidding me," Heather said, her perfectly shaped lips crumpling in a dubious frown.

"No." *Mum's the word*, Danielle thought. The girls were dying for an explanation, and she would enjoy watching them squirm.

"No?" Teresa repeated. "Just *no*?" She flicked her fingers over the surface of the water, sending a splash in Danielle's direction. "Come on, Danielle. We want details!"

"Lots of juicy, spicy details!" Heather agreed, more curious than ever.

Condescending laughter danced from Danielle's lips. "No," she repeated with a jolt of satisfaction.

Now frantic with curiosity, Heather and Teresa exchanged a desperate look.

"All you need to know is that—" Danielle hesitated. "Well, Don and I did set off some fireworks last night—even if no one else was around to see the explosion."

That nearly blasted them out of the water. For once Danielle had managed to render her friends speechless.

"Yes," Danielle continued, "Merivale's hottest romance is still crackling. In fact, there's so much electricity in the air, I wouldn't be surprised if all the fuses in town blow out the next time Don and I get together."

"Ooooh!" Teresa squealed.

Heather let out a slow whistle. "Hot stuff! You sly girl!"

Satisfied with the spoils of another victory, Danielle closed her eyes and leaned back. With an occasional smile or nod, she pretended to listen as her friends filled her in on the details of last night's party.

But her mind was churning as swiftly as the jet streams in the hot tub. The girls were impressed with her story—for now. But sooner or later they would need to see some proof that Don was crazy in love with her. And that would be tricky, as long as he was living in dread with his parents.

Her work was cut out for her, but Danielle thrived on the thrill of a challenge. Soon Don's parent troubles would be over. She would make sure of that. And then Don would be free to concentrate on her—twenty-four hours a day.

Because, once again, Danielle had a cunning, brilliant, slightly devious plan. And Danielle Sharp always got her man.

Snip-snip-snip.
A smile lit Lori Randall's face as she applied the finishing touches to a new outfit.

A golden shaft of morning sunlight streamed through her bedroom, and the sweet aroma of freshly baked cinnamon rolls lured her downstairs.

But when she had woken up that morning, her latest creation had cried out for completion—and Lori just couldn't resist. Besides, this miniskirt would be perfect for today's warm weather.

The faded denim of the skirt felt unusually soft as she trimmed the loose threads along the hemline. The pale cornflower-blue shade was just right—the result of soaking the coarse material in bleach overnight, then washing it with fabric softener.

With a tremor of anticipation she slipped on the skirt and fastened the row of decorative buckles over her right hip.

Outrageous! She twirled around in front of the mirror, giddy with delight. The miniskirt revealed an enticing glimpse of her shapely legs, and the soft shade seemed to highlight the healthy glow of her fair skin and sky-blue eyes.

But the greatest thrill was in the creation. She'd taken another design from sketch to completion, and she was pleased with the results.

I'm on my way, she thought as she slipped on a bubble-gum pink T-shirt and raced down the stairs. Someday she would be a famous fashion designer. But right now her immediate priority was snagging one of her mom's delicious cinnamon rolls.

"Good morning, Lori," her father called while on his way out of the kitchen. Armed with a cup of coffee and the Sunday papers, George Randall was headed for the living room to catch up on the news.

"Hi, Dad. Do you have the fashion section there?"

Mr. Randall juggled the newspapers so that Lori could extract the section she wanted.

"Thanks." She dropped it onto the kitchen table and went to pour a glass of orange juice.

"There's a sale on at D. B. Durant's," her mother said, looking up from the Sunday circular of specials at Merivale Mall. "Cute outfit."

"Thanks." Pleased, Lori sat down at the table, bit into a cinnamon roll, and eagerly leafed through her favorite section of the Sunday paper. An article on hats featured photos of turbans, pillbox hats, boaters, and berets.

The photograph of the beret reminded Lori of Nora Pringle, and the cruel boys who'd snatched her hat last night.

"Do you know Nora Pringle?" she asked her mother. When Mrs. Randall shook her head, Lori added, "You know, that poor lady who spends most of her time at Merivale Mall? The one with all the shopping bags and raggedy clothes. She usually wears a purple beret."

As it turned out, Cynthia Randall did recall seeing the unfortunate woman at the mall. And the expression on her face sharpened with concern when Lori described the incident between Nora and the gang.

"Those goofball kids." Lori's mother shook her head. "I know they're basically harmless, but it's sad that they get their kicks from harassing that poor woman."

Lori nodded as she swallowed a bite of her roll. "They were pretty obnoxious, but the whole thing made me start thinking about Nora Pringle. She's all alone in the world, with no family and no home—not even a dime to her name." Her blue eyes glimmered with determination. "I want to help her, Mom."

Mrs. Randall put aside the newspaper ads and focused on her daughter. "I'm sure you do, dear, but it's not always easy to help someone in need. How well do you actually know Miss Pringle?"

"I see her nearly every day. She's like a fixture at Merivale Mall."

"But how well do you really know her? Have you ever spoken with her? Asked her about her home and family?"

"No." Lori shrugged. "I don't know her that well. And I never wanted to pry—"

"Because you respect her privacy," Mrs. Randall finished for her daughter. "That's understandable. But maybe Nora Pringle has a home she doesn't like. Maybe she has a family and people who love her. Maybe she just chooses to live on her own, independently."

How could anyone leave their family to live on a hard bench in the middle of a public mall? Lori found it hard to believe that Nora had a choice. No, she thought. Nora Pringle was a desperate, lonely woman. She was sure of that.

Lori's mother sighed before she continued. "And there are a few other considerations too. Everyone is entitled to their pride—no matter how they live. Nora may be too proud to accept anything from you."

A smile lit Lori's face. "I thought about that. So I decided to help Nora get back on her feet. If I can find her a job, she'll never have to accept charity—or pick through a garbage can—ever again."

"I don't know . . ." Mrs. Randall still seemed skeptical. In the course of her nursing career, she had had numerous experiences with homeless, poverty-stricken people. And since she specialized in care of the elderly, she frequently encountered senile or mentally ill patients.

"Don't you have some friends who specialize in cases like Nora's?" Lori persisted.

Her mother nodded. "And you should certainly give this thing your best shot, but don't be too disappointed if Miss Pringle resists your help. Homeless people can be difficult to deal with. Sometimes they're insulted by the idea of charity. Sometimes they're suffering from mental illness. Nora may not be able to even carry on a rational conversation with you."

Cynthia Randall began to search through the kitchen drawers until she found her address book. "I'll give you the number of a social service agency here in Merivale. It's run by a woman named Mimi Turner, an old friend of mine from nursing school. If anyone can help Nora, it's Mimi."

Lori watched over her mother's shoulder as she jotted down the agency's phone number.

"I'm proud of you for trying to help," Mrs. Randall added. "Just don't get your hopes up too high."

Lori nodded. "I'll try not to." But deep in her heart she knew she wouldn't rest until she'd helped make Nora Pringle's world a little better.

CHAPTER FIVE

"Donald, your father doesn't like it when you monopolize the phone."

The shrill voice rang over the telephone line, rattling Danielle's nerves. *"Who is that?"* she asked Don.

"My mother," he muttered into the receiver. "She makes me feel like a two-year-old."

Danielle shifted the phone to her other ear. She was a little shocked by Mrs. James's rude interruption. Her own mother did her share of complaining, but Serena Sharp would be appalled if anyone outside the family heard it.

"Look," Don said. "I'd better go before she starts hounding me again."

"No . . . wait! Are we on for that movie tonight?"

When there was only a long silence over the telephone wire, Danielle fought off a surge of irritation. Since Don had moved in with his parents three days earlier, she hadn't seen him once. *I might as well be dating the man on the moon, considering all the time we spend together!*

"I don't know, Red," Don finally answered. "Things are so messed up right now, I'm not sure I could even concentrate on a flick."

"Then why don't you come over to my house? We can hang out and talk, just like last Saturday—"

"No dice, Red. I'm afraid I'd make rotten company tonight."

Danielle's heart sank as his words cut her to the quick. Don didn't understand how eager she was to see him, even if he was still depressed and distracted. How could she help him if she couldn't even get near him?

"Listen, Don," she began, "I realize that—"

"*Donald . . .*"—Mrs. James's voice was an annoying whine—"*get off the phone—now!*"

"Gotta go, Red. She's on the rampage again. I'll talk to you . . . soon," he promised.

Nestled on the white leather sofa in her bedroom, Danielle held the receiver away from her ear, staring at it until the line went dead.

Nothing was going according to plan. All week long she'd been trying to finagle an invitation to Don's house, trying to see Don, trying to figure out a way to meet his infamous parents. If she could analyze Mr. and Mrs. James, she could diagnose their weak and strong points. And then she'd be in a better position to help Don.

But it was time to scrap her original plan. If she waited for Don to come around, she'd end up waiting till her hair turned gray. The digital clock on the nightstand said 4:52 P.M.— nearly dinnertime. Time to take action.

If Don couldn't come to her, she would go to him.

After all, wasn't she a true master at manipulation? Danielle Sharp was Merivale's number-one expert at getting her way.

Just as quickly as she dreamed up a new scheme, she began to set it in motion. She sprang to her feet, pulled on a pair of teal suede boots with a low-cut cuff, and snatched up her car keys from the top of her dresser.

When you operated in a war zone, it was important to have an alternative strategy.

This was the block. The rows of modest ranch houses looked so tacky with their tiny square lawns and meager gardens, Danielle thought. She was willing to suffer the mediocrity of a middle-class neighborhood to be close to Don.

Passing his parents' house, she drove up the next block, then let her car coast to a stop just a few inches away from the curb.

Since Don was an ace mechanic, this breakdown couldn't look too obvious. And it couldn't be too easy to fix, either. Otherwise Don would have the engine of her BMW purring in no time, and her plan wouldn't have a chance.

What should she tamper with? Danielle stared at the motor under the hood of the BMW. For such an expensive car, it looked awfully dirty. Didn't her father's mechanic ever clean this engine?

Danielle bit her lip as she studied the clutter of hoses and metal casings. She didn't know where to begin. Finally, a plastic container of blue liquid seemed like a likely victim.

With a devious smile she found a metal nail file in her purse and started poking the container. When nothing happened she yanked on a tube near the bottom. After a few tugs the tube snapped, and blue liquid spilled onto the street.

Stage one was completed.

Now for stage two—sweetening the sour disposition of Don's parents.

Danielle brushed away a grimy smudge on one hand as she headed toward the James's house. Although this stage was a bit more complicated, it was destined for success.

Who could resist a polite girl friend with a smile as sweet as maple sugar?

"Whatever it is you're selling, we're not interested."

Danielle recognized the shrill voice of Don's mother, but she barely got a glimpse inside before the woman began to swing the front door closed again.

"I'm sorry to bother you, Mrs. James," she said quickly and politely, "but my car broke down on the next block, and I thought that maybe Don could take a look at it. I'm a good friend of his . . . Danielle Sharp."

The petite woman didn't slam the door, but she didn't invite Danielle in, either. With a curious gaze she eyed Danielle from head to toe. "Wait here," she said, then disappeared into the darkness beyond the screen door.

Not the most cordial introduction, Danielle thought, but she would have to give the woman a chance to warm up to her.

A moment later Don appeared in the doorway. "Red, what are you doing here?" His black hair was slightly disheveled, giving him a wild, reckless appearance.

With a rush of emotion Danielle suddenly remembered how well this guy could read her every move. Don would never fall for this little trick . . . but there was no backing out now.

"My car broke down about a block away. I was going to call the auto club, but when I realized you lived so close by, I thought that—"

"Sure, Red." Don smiled, putting a halt to her babbled explanation. "I'll take a look. Come on in." He held the door open for her.

Danielle walked into the living room and sat down on the sofa, trying not to stare at the unfortunate decor. The house was clean and neat, stuffed with oversized Mediterranean furniture. But Mrs. James had made some poor choices in design, and the total effect was so . . . déclassé.

At first Danielle didn't even notice the tall, lanky man parked in the easy chair. He was facing the television set, seemingly hypnotized by the evening news. "Oh, hi there." Danielle flashed the man a stunning smile.

"That's my father," Don said. "Dad, this is Danielle Sharp, a friend of mine."

"How do?" Waving in Danielle's direction, Mr. James didn't even bother to look away from the TV screen.

While Don ducked into the kitchen, Danielle tried to make small talk with Mr. James. But Don's father refused to be distracted from the boob tube. He merely grunted or nodded whenever she asked him a polite question.

Mr. James was lost in his own little world. How was Danielle going to impress him when she couldn't even capture his attention?

Danielle nibbled at her glossed lip as she mulled over the problem. So far she'd done a fabulous job playing the polite, dutiful girl friend. Sooner or later one of Don's parents would recognize her wonderful qualities. Other kids' parents were always putty in Danielle's hands.

"Would you like something to drink, Danielle?" Mrs. James called from the kitchen.

"Yes, please." Danielle smiled. Now, this was more like it! She would strike up a friendly conversation when Danielle's mother returned with her drink.

But Mrs. James never reappeared. Two commercials later Don walked in with a glass of ginger ale. "Here you go. How far away is your car?"

"Just down the block." As Danielle took a sip, she began to wonder about the wisdom of her plan. The Jameses didn't seem at all enthralled by her visit. In fact, they looked annoyed. And Don seemed uncomfortable, sitting like a statue in his parents' living room.

"How did the trouble start?" Don asked.

Danielle glanced down at a telltale grease smudge on the back of her hand. "I was driving along on a side street, when all of a sudden this—this blue stuff started dripping from the engine."

Don's eyebrows shot up. "Blue stuff? From under the—"

"Shhh! The news is coming on," Mr. James interrupted.

As Don fell silent, Danielle understood. She knew how it felt to be invisible in your own home. Don seemed like an intruder in his parents' house—which wasn't a happy place to begin with. The tension in the air was so thick, you could almost cut it with a knife.

By the time Danielle finished her ginger ale, she had abandoned her new scheme. There was no way Don's parents could be charmed or controlled. She would have to come up with another plan, working around Don's parents.

Eager to bolt out of the dingy, stuffy house, Danielle sat on the sofa waiting for a sign from Don. When at last he stood up, she went into the kitchen and thanked Mrs. James for the drink.

"You're quite welcome," Mrs. James murmured. When Don's mother glanced up, Danielle noticed gray circles underneath her eyes. For a moment she almost felt sorry for the weary woman. But that feeling faded as soon as she stepped back into the living room.

"Just because you have to fix her car," Mrs. James sniped at Don, "doesn't mean you're out for the night. I want you back in one hour. Youngsters your age shouldn't be wandering the streets at night."

Youngsters? Danielle couldn't believe her ears. Don was seventeen years old!

Despite his reckless looks and rowdy friends, Don was one of the most mature guys Danielle knew. He split his time between school and a part-time job at a local garage. He was the town hero since he'd saved that kid at Merivale Mall. And yet his own parents treated him like a child.

* * *

Laced with a silky breeze, the cool evening air washed over Danielle, bringing freedom and relief. She followed Don down the street, struck by the strong lines of his handsome profile against the red sky.

Another plan had backfired, and she wasn't sure what to do next. The injustice of the situation stung her, making her hurt for Don. After all these years, why did Mr. and Mrs. James have the right to rule his life? Why didn't they just leave him alone?

He looked back at her, his eyes dark and unreadable. "Don't let them get to you. They're just messed up over money and stuff." He took her hand and squeezed it reassuringly just before they reached her car.

As soon as he looked under the hood, Don discovered the problem. "It's just the windshield cleaning fluid. Looks like it's been . . ." Mercifully, his voice trailed off as he leaned closer to the engine.

"Is it serious, Dr. James?" Danielle asked, giving the BMW's fender a concerned pat.

"Nothing to worry about." Don backed away from the car, wiping his palms on his jeans. "In fact, it shouldn't affect the way the car runs at all." He leaned inside the car and turned the key in the ignition. Immediately, the engine roared to life. A suspicious frown settled on his face. "Runs like a charm. Didn't you say that the car was broken down?"

"Well . . ." Of all things! She'd drained the stupid windshield cleaner. But the container was so big and prominent, it had looked important. "Maybe that blue stuff drowned the engine," she suggested, tossing a strand of fiery red hair over her shoulder. She had to think of a way out of this mess—and fast! "You know, Don, you're a whiz when it comes to this engine stuff."

He smiled. "Yeah. But it doesn't take a genius to figure this one out."

Ready to protest, Danielle stuck her hands on her hips and gave him a lethal look. But Don was already leaning under the hood again, so she let the subject drop.

Don closed the hood. "Let's give it a test run." He slid into the driver's seat next to Danielle and put the car in gear.

For a while they drove without talking, listening to the radio and the rustle of the wind whipping in through the open sunroof. When *Stardust Dreams* started playing, Danielle's heart swelled with sadness. This song always made her think of Don. She'd planned to share it with him in a wonderful, perfect moment.

But this was all wrong. Don was miserable, and she was so confused.

"*Every time I see your face . . . stardust dreams . . .*"

It should have been a romantic moment, but Don's face was shadowed with a tired look.

"I see what you mean about your parents," Danielle said. "It must be murder living with them."

"It is. My father's been out of work for six months now. He doesn't know what to do with himself. Loses his temper sometimes. But most of the time he sits around brooding. My mother used to leave him alone. But now that money's getting tight, they've been sniping at each other. And at me."

Don pulled the BMW over to the side of the road, but he continued to stare straight ahead. "They're driving me crazy, Red. I've been trying to stay cool, but I'm beginning to lose it."

He gripped the steering wheel so tightly, his knuckles were white. "Something's got to give. Every day it gets worse instead of better."

When he turned to Danielle, his eyes glimmered. "I don't know what to do, Red."

"It's so unfair." The corners of Danielle's perfectly shaped lips turned down in a pout. "They don't seem to want you there, but they refuse to let you live on your own. Isn't there someone else—another relative you could stay with for the next year or so?"

"No." Don shook his head. "Just good old Mom and Dad."

"Home sweet home," she muttered.

Don laughed. "I always knew you were a good judge of character." He brushed a tendril of coppery hair from her shoulder, then ran his fingers up to her smooth cheek.

His touch made Danielle quiver inside. She struggled to stay cool as he lifted her chin, bringing her face close to his.

"And after all this, you've still got a sense of humor. I like that about you, Red."

"And when you hold me close . . . stardust dreams . . ."

When he kissed her, she knew she'd lost the battle. Calm, cool, collected Danielle Sharp slipped into another world whenever a certain guy held her in his arms. Don's kisses filled her with wonderful sweeping feelings, emotions she wished she could lock away in a secret place. These were the feelings a girl would want to cherish for the rest of her life.

"And, Red," Don whispered in her ear. "Next time you want to see me, just tell me. Your car won't survive much more of this."

CHAPTER SIX

"I'm sorry, Lori, but there's nothing we can do until your friend comes in and applies for aid."

With her pink Trimline phone to her ear, Lori listened carefully as Mimi Turner explained the agency's policies. The woman's voice sounded kind enough, but Lori found the news disheartening.

Sitting cross-legged on her bed, Lori twisted the phone cord around her fingers as she spoke. "The problem is," she explained to the social worker, "I don't think Miss Pringle will come in to apply personally. She's very shy, and she seems kind of embarrassed about accepting help from strangers."

54

A wistful expression crossed Lori's face as she remembered that Saturday night in the loading docks. Nora had disappeared so suddenly, as if she were afraid even of Lori—a five foot five wisp of a blonde!

Even though a few days had passed, Lori still couldn't erase the image of the frightened woman from her mind. She couldn't forget how Nora had looked cowering behind those boxes, her eyes wide with fear. She just had to help that feeble woman!

"What if I came in and applied for her?" Lori's voice lightened with a new glimmer of hope. "Or maybe I could just pick up the application forms and bring them to her?"

"I'm afraid this is one rule we can't bend. It's the law," Mimi Turner said apologetically. "We have to interview each client to make sure that financial assistance goes to the people who truly need it."

Lori frowned. "I understand—I guess." But what about the needy people who were too proud or too scared to apply?

The woman's voice softened. "I can appreciate Miss Pringle's feelings, but my hands are tied. Tell her that we're open five days a week, and that we're here to help people like her. You can give her this number if you like."

"Thanks, Ms. Turner," Lori said. "I'll do my best to coax Nora into your office."

"I know you will. Nora Pringle is lucky to have a friend like you."

Lori said good-bye and hung up with a sigh. Her task wasn't going to be easy. First of all, she wasn't quite sure how to locate Nora Pringle. After being harassed by those boys, the poor woman might stay in hiding forever.

But Lori wasn't going to give up. Every time she thought about the homeless woman, her determination burned brighter, like a furious fire.

If Nora Pringle needed help, Lori knew exactly who to call.

Picking up a familiar old stuffed animal, she tucked him under one arm and used her other hand to punch in Patsy Donovan's phone number.

"Hello, Pats? It's Lori. Hold on to your hat, 'cause we've got a bi-i-ig problem. . . ."

The next day Danielle faced her own set of problems when she met her friends for lunch.

"So what's the latest on you and Don?" Teresa asked, wagging a carrot sliver at Danielle. "Are things sizzling . . . or fizzling?"

"Yeah," Heather added, flicking her glossy black hair back over one delicate ear. "I'm beginning to wonder if this so-called romance is just a legend in your own mind."

Danielle clutched her drinking straw tightly, stabbing at the ice in her cup as her friends cracked up. Let them laugh, she thought. They wouldn't know a hot romance if it singed their fingers.

But the brittle sound of their laughter seemed to ring throughout Atwood's cafeteria. Danielle glanced over her shoulder. Was it just her imagination, or were people looking over at her, wondering if she was actually a reject—a dateless failure?

"Some girls prefer not to kiss and tell," she snapped with a green-eyed glare.

Her two friends exchanged suspicious glances.

"Oh, come on," Teresa insisted. "You've never been shy before. And we know you're not modest about your fantastic conquests. You were supposed to go to the movies with Donny-boy last night. What gives?"

Majestically, Heather raised her hand to stop Teresa's interrogation. "If Danielle's not talking, maybe it's because there's nothing to tell. . . ."

Livid with anger, Danielle gritted her teeth. She could feel the blood rushing to her face, flawing her perfect complexion. Of course there was something to tell! There was magic—frantic and furious—every time Don held her in his arms.

But these girls didn't want to hear about his mother's meat loaf or a few stolen kisses in the dark. They were primed for glamour, glitz and excitement. They'd never be satisfied with the truth, but Danielle couldn't let them think that her romance was all washed up.

"Did you or did you not go to the movies?" Teresa prodded.

"The movies?" Danielle echoed. "Boy, was I wrong about that date."

Heather's slate-blue eyes narrowed suspiciously.

"So . . . tell us!" Teresa demanded.

"Well," Danielle purred, "when I opened the front door and found Don waiting there with an armful of roses, I knew the night was too special to waste on a movie."

"*Don James* brought you *roses*?" Heather's voice was tainted with doubt.

"Long-stemmed," Danielle said, embellishing the lie. "My room is filled with their fragrance." *Let them swallow that line*, she thought with a satisfied smile.

"Flowers, huh?" A skeptical look darkened Teresa's chocolate-brown eyes. "And then what? Did you go to the Video Arcade for a Star Command tournament?"

Heather and Teresa burst into giggles.

"Very funny." Danielle had a strong urge to wipe those smug little smirks off their faces. "Although that may be *your* idea of a fun date, Don and I have more sophisticated tastes. He took me to dinner at a tiny country inn . . . tucked in the woods . . . showered with moonlight." Romantic images rolled off her tongue before she could restrain herself.

"A country inn? Where?" Heather probed.

"It's . . . it's very small and exclusive, hidden at the end of a winding road . . . just off Route 32. Afterward, we went for a stroll along the shore of a nearby pond. The moon cast a silver glow over the water, and the sky was studded with millions of sparkling stars. . . ."

As Danielle's voice trailed off, she stole a quick glance at her friends. They seemed to be weakening, but she could tell that they still didn't buy the whole story.

"Well, wonders never cease," Heather said, then delicately popped a single raisin into her mouth. "This certainly doesn't sound like the Don James I know."

"Maybe he took a dating refresher course," Teresa sniped.

Danielle masked her annoyance with a casual shrug. "Believe whatever you want. What do I care. I'm the one with the perfect boyfriend."

She plucked a handful of raisins from Heather's bag, all the while assessing her friends' reactions. "You know, Don is really a sensitive romantic at heart. I guess he just needed the right girl to bring out his best qualities."

At last the girls seemed to be on the verge of believing her. Something about Danielle's I-don't-care-what-you-think attitude had con-

vinced them that she really had something cooking with Don.

"Verrry interesting," Heather murmured.

Brushing a tiny crumb from her silk blouse,
Teresa admitted, "Sounds pretty wild. But how
can you ever top that? What's next on the agenda
for Merivale's hottest sweethearts?"

Time to think fast! Danielle had to come up
with a dream date that would knock everyone's
socks off! Stalling for a moment, she fluffed her
coppery hair and let a mournful sigh escape her
lips.

"Well," she answered, "sometimes I'm afraid
Merivale just doesn't have enough to offer two
people like Don and me. Romantically speaking, of course."

"Of course," Heather echoed as Teresa nodded eagerly.

"So . . . for our next date, we're going out
of town—to Philadelphia!" she announced, suddenly inspired. "We've got tickets for the Bad
Boys' concert at the Spectrum. Don arranged it
all as a surprise for me. Wasn't that sweet of
him?"

"The Bad Boys!" Teresa's mouth dropped
so far open, Danielle felt sure her jaw would hit
the floor.

"The guys who do *Stardust Dreams*?" Heather
exclaimed. "I adore that song."

"Not to mention the hunks in the band,"
Teresa added with a wink.

"But Philadelphia?" Heather looked skeptical. "Will your parents let you go on an out-of-town date?"

"What they don't know won't hurt them." Danielle's smile revealed a row of perfect white teeth straightened by years of braces. "My parents will be away for the weekend. They'll never know what time I get back from Philly—if I decide to come back at all!"

"It sounds totally wicked!" Teresa exclaimed. "Wicked—but wonderful."

"Doesn't it?" said Danielle. If only it were true! She'd told such a convincing tale, she'd nearly conned herself. The idea of a romantic weekend with Don—traveling to Philly, seeing the Bad Boys in concert, making *Stardust Dreams* their song—left her squirming with delight.

She had created such a fantastic lie. How could she ever face the tumble back to reality? And after the weekend passed without a dream date, how would she ever explain this whopper to her best friends?

The consequences of her latest lie plagued Danielle all afternoon, niggling at the back of her mind.

Madame DuChamps called on her in French class, and she was so preoccupied that she flubbed her answer. The whole class burst into laughter when Danielle said, in French, "I like to eat my bike." She was mortified.

When the final bell rang at last, Danielle jumped into her white BMW and headed toward her personal shrine, Merivale Mall. In the sunny, clean atmosphere of the mall, surrounded by all the fabulous delights money could buy, Danielle always felt at home.

As the brass-trimmed door closed behind her, Danielle peered out the glass bubble of the central elevator. Below her sprawled the empire her father had built, the finest playground any teenage girl could ever dream of.

The elevator whooshed her above the first level, and she noticed her cousin Lori standing beside the fountain, talking with a group of friends. The sight of Lori in that ugly orange and yellow waitress uniform made Danielle cringe. It was bad enough that her cousin needed to work. But the fact that she had a job in the midst of Danielle's favorite hangout only rubbed salt in the wound.

Although Lori was a good kid, she reminded Danielle of a world she'd left behind years before. And Danielle liked to keep her distance, for fear that her middle-class childhood would someday catch up with her.

Snazzz! Shoe Hut. The Magic Factory. The illuminated signs of the stores on the second level flashed past her as the elevator zoomed upward. Preferring to shop in the expensive boutiques, Danielle usually made a beeline for the fourth level.

Whipping past the third floor, she noticed a sandwich-board sign on the midway. BENSON'S —YOUR TICKET TO THE BAD BOYS! Then the elevator whirred to a halt on the top level.

"That's it!" she shrieked, startling a woman who'd begun to corral her kids off the elevator.

Rushing back to the third level, Danielle congratulated herself on finding a solution. Her fantastic lie could become a reality if she and Don actually went to the concert in Philly!

One of two department stores in Merivale Mall, Benson's featured an outlet that sold tickets to major concerts and sporting events. But since the Bad Boys were a rock and roll sensation, there was a good chance that their concert was completely sold out.

Please have tickets left! Please, please, please! Danielle prayed as she approached the ticket window.

"You're very lucky, miss," the clerk told her from behind a glass partition. "That concert is nearly sold out. We've got a few choice seats available at $37.50, and then there are a few nosebleed specials in the top rows, selling at—"

"I'll take them," Danielle said breathlessly, sliding her credit card through the slot. "The best seats you've got for Saturday night."

Danielle's heart drummed as the clerk typed

the information into the computer. A moment later the machine spewed out two concert tickets.

"Thanks." She nearly ripped them out of the clerk's hand. These were her tickets to happiness, her tickets to popularity.

This weekend Danielle Sharp would go down in Merivale romance history. She and Don would have a great time, and Heather and Teresa could stew in their jealousy.

Tucking the tickets into her stamped leather bag, she headed for the Video Arcade on the first level of the mall. She wanted to tell Don about their exciting weekend, and she had a hunch she'd find him behind the controls of Astro-Blasters.

There was a lift in Danielle's step as she sauntered through Merivale Mall. She felt happy to be beautiful, in love, and in possession of several shiny plastic charge cards.

Shopping could be sheer bliss!

CHAPTER SEVEN

"We don't have much time," Lori Randall told her friends. From where she was standing beside a fountain, she didn't even notice as her cousin Danielle raced by and ducked into the entrance of the Video Arcade.

Lori's mind was focused on an important matter—namely, Project Pringle.

As Patsy Donovan checked her watch, her cookie-shaped hat slipped down over her reddish-brown curls. "I've got to be back at work in thirty minutes." Patsy worked at the Cookie Connection, only two doors down from Tio's Tacos.

"I hope we can find her quickly," Ann Larson said.

"So do I." Lori was concerned because she hadn't seen Miss Pringle since last Saturday. And Lori spent a lot of time in Merivale Mall— thirty hours a week at Tio's Tacos.

"These walkie-talkies were a great idea, Lori." Patsy pressed the button on hers and spoke into the mouthpiece, testing it. "They'll save us a lot of time—over and out."

"You're coming through loud and clear," Ann said with a smile.

"Teddy wasn't too happy about surrendering his favorite toy, until I explained why we wanted to borrow it." Lori had finally talked her eleven-year-old brother into loaning her his walkie-talkie set. The radios would help the girls communicate while they searched the mall.

"Gee." Patsy flicked the radio's button back and forth. "I feel like one of those private detectives on TV."

"Thanks for helping me out," Lori told her two best friends. "It might take me forever to find her on my own."

"What are friends for?" Patsy teased.

"We'll give it our best shot." Ann seemed to radiate encouragement. Her wavy chestnut hair was caught up in a neat French braid in preparation for another workout session. "If we don't find her now, I can help you look later— after my last class."

"No go." Lori shook her head, her blue eyes solemn. "I have to work at Tio's until closing. Just remember, if you find Nora Pringle, don't rush her. She's probably still wary after that incident with those boys."

Patsy and Ann nodded. When Lori had telephoned her friends last night, she'd told them each everything she knew about Nora Pringle. Both girls shared Lori's concern about the feeble, desolate woman.

Lori had planned to enlist Nick's help, too, but he'd been so busy. Nick had been spending most evenings at the library submerged in research for a history paper. When Lori saw how involved his project was, she didn't have the heart to distract him with her problems.

"Why don't we each take a different floor," Ann suggested. "I can start at the top and work my way down. Patsy can start on level two—"

"And I'll cover the loading docks, then work my way up," Lori chimed in.

"Check," Patsy said, pushing her cookie hat back with the antenna of her walkie-talkie. "Are we ready to roll?"

"Ten-four." Lori smiled at her friends. "Let's step on it, Mugsy."

Ann rolled her gray eyes. "You guys are beginning to sound less like detectives and more like gangsters!"

"I just checked out Facades and I'm on my way to High Hats," Ann reported over the air. "No sign of Nora yet."

Next came Patsy's voice. "Fifty percent off jeans at the Pants Patio—but no Miss Pringle."

Shoving a carton aside, Lori checked a dark cubbyhole. But there was no sign of life in the sub-basement of the mall. "Nothing to report from the loading docks—though it looks like a few crates of chocolate bars just arrived for the cinema snack bar."

"My mouth is watering," Ann said. "Can you beam one up?" Ann was a chocolate fanatic.

"Sorry, Ann. My telepathic chocolate powers are on the fritz today."

"There's a new salesclerk at the Pen and Paper," Patsy reported. "And he's a super hunk. I think he's the surfer who just moved to Merivale from southern California—"

"Patsy," Ann interrupted. "It would break Irv's heart to see you ogling a beach bum."

Irv Zalaznick was Patsy's boyfriend, one of the sweetest guys in Merivale, she always said.

"You're right," Patsy agreed. "No ogling beach bums—but no sign of Nora."

As Lori finished searching the loading docks, she felt a twinge of disappointment. She'd hoped to find Nora, tucked away in her favorite place.

"All clear on the underground level," she transmitted to her friends. "I'm heading upstairs."

"Meet you on the first floor," Patsy added. "I'm through with the second level."

"And I'm heading down to three," Ann reported. "I'll keep you posted."

Refusing to be discouraged, Lori picked up the tempo of her search. Stopping into each store, she spoke to salesclerks and managers. The more she spread the word about Nora, the more aware people would be of the woman's isolation. It certainly wouldn't hurt for the people of Merivale Mall to pitch in and help the needy woman.

But every time Lori recited her little speech, people just shrugged off her questions.

"Sorry, miss. I've never seen her," said one clerk.

"The owner doesn't allow her in here," whispered the cashier at O'Burgers. "He's afraid she'll scare off the other customers."

"But Nora wouldn't hurt a flea!" Lori protested.

The girl nodded. "Oh, I know the old lady's harmless." She lowered her voice. "But it's the owner's policy."

The search proved fruitless, and time was running out. The girls had to report back to their jobs—they couldn't afford to be late. By the time Lori met her friends back at the fountain, she'd heard an earful of myths about Nora Pringle.

"What an eye opener!" she told the girls. "You wouldn't believe the outrageous stories people have made up about that poor woman. One kid told me that he thinks Nora's mumbling to alien beings from outer space!"

Ann was indignant. "That's ridiculous!"

"People say the darnedest things!" Patsy agreed.

Lori folded up the antenna on her walkie-talkie. "I guess people need to make up explanations for things they don't understand." She frowned. "I'm just surprised everyone doesn't recognize the truth—that Nora is a poor, lonely old lady."

Patsy and Ann exchanged a concerned look.

"Don't let it get you down, Lori," said Patsy. "She'll turn up soon. And I'm sure she's fine. Nora's a survivor, right?"

After a moment of thought Lori smiled. "Right."

"Sorry we couldn't do more." Ann handed her walkie-talkie back to Lori. "But I've got to skedaddle if I'm going to teach my class."

"You two were a big help." Lori gathered the radios in her arms. "Thanks a mill."

"We can try again this weekend," Patsy suggested as she straightened the skirt of her uniform. "I have to work, but I can look for Nora during breaks."

"Good idea!" Lori was encouraged by her friends' support. "But right now we'd better get to work—before we all land in a heap of trouble!"

For the third time that afternoon Danielle ducked into the Video Arcade in search of Don James.

It hadn't bothered her when he wasn't there the first time she'd checked. There were plenty of things for Danielle to do at Merivale Mall.

High Hats was having a sale on leather miniskirts with exquisite buttery-soft textures. And she was running out of Fallen Angel. D. B. Durant's carried the sumptuous perfume for $100 a half-ounce. It was atrociously expensive but worth every penny as far as Danielle was concerned. She deserved it!

She paused a moment, waiting for her eyes to adjust to the semidarkness and flashing lights of the arcade. Where was Don?

On most days he hung out at the Video Arcade. But now that he was nowhere to be found, Danielle began to wonder if something was up. Was Don trapped at home—forever?

Danielle was getting impatient. She wanted to settle their weekend date, but she wasn't about to drive out to that dragon's lair he called home. She'd had enough of Mr. and Mrs. James to last her a lifetime.

A cluster of guys dressed in black leather jackets and faded jeans caught her eye. Two of them were sitting on an old pinball machine, their legs casually slung over the side. The third kid stood before them, talking in a low voice.

They were Don's friends, members of a rowdy motorcycle gang. Danielle had seen her boyfriend hanging out with these guys on a few occasions. But where was Don?

As if on cue, Don sauntered up to the group and nudged one guy on the shoulder. "Thought I'd find you degenerates hanging out here," Don said with a chuckle.

Danielle's heart lifted at the sight of him. With his dark coloring and lean build, Don was absolutely gorgeous! If only he were more discriminating when it came to choosing friends!

Taking a deep, calming breath, she stepped forward just enough to capture Don's attention.

His eyes seemed to glimmer when he spotted her. "See if you can stay out of trouble for two seconds," he told his friends as he backed away.

Danielle flashed him a coy smile, aiming to melt his heart. But her plan backfired the minute Don took her arm and led her toward a wall of vending machines. His dark gaze turned all her resolve to jelly.

"What's up, Red?" He pumped a few coins into a soft-drink machine and pulled out a can of soda.

Quickly, breathlessly, Danielle explained about the Bad Boys' concert in Philadelphia. Don listened, thoughtfully considering the excursion as he sipped from the can.

"The seats I bought are great—and the show's almost sold out!"

Don nodded, swallowing a swig of soda. "Sounds pretty cool."

A spark of hope flickered in Danielle's emerald eyes. "So . . . that means you'll take me?"

"Sure." Don shrugged. "Why not?"

Perfect! "We'll have to leave by five if we want to make the beginning of the concert." Already new plans were clicking into place in Danielle's cunning mind. "And we can go to dinner afterward—someplace utterly outrageous. I wonder if we can get reservations at—"

"Hey, James," called one of Don's friends. "You ready to go, man?"

"In a minute, Zack." Don looked back at Danielle. "Sorry, Red. Got things to do. But we're on for Saturday. I'll meet you at your place around—"

"Five o'clock—sharp!" she finished. "But wait! What's your hurry? You've been hard to find lately. Something secretive going on?"

"Just something I've been working on with Zack and the guys."

"A car engine?" she probed.

Don laughed. "Not exactly. I'll tell you about it some other time. Right now Zack's getting antsy to leave. Catch you Saturday," Don said, squeezing her arm before he walked off to join his friends.

His touch sent shards of sensation tingling through her veins. Forcing a smile, Danielle hoped her emotions weren't showing on her face. She didn't want Don to know how she yearned to throw herself into his arms!

*　　*　　*

At last the dinner rush was over. Sponge in hand, Lori was wiping a stubborn smudge from the counter at Tio's when she heard a familiar voice.

"Nick Hobart reporting for duty, ma'am."

The sponge slipped from Lori's fingers as the sound of his voice warmed her heart. "Nick! What are you doing here?"

"Is that any way to greet your boyfriend?" Nick teased, pushing back the white leather sleeves of his Cougar jacket. "Besides, I'm here to pick up my assignment for Project Pringle."

"How did you find out about that?" Hands on her hips, Lori tilted her head up to get a better look at him.

More than six feet tall, Nick sometimes seemed to tower over her. His golden-brown hair was ever so slightly touseled by the wind. Lori had to stop herself from staring. Sometimes she couldn't believe her own good fortune. Nick Hobart, heartthrob and star quarterback of Atwood Academy, was really and truly her boyfriend!

"Project Pringle, huh?" Lori folded her arms in front of her. "I'm afraid that's top-secret information. Especially for guys who have monster research papers due on Monday."

"Is that why I was left out?" A frown settled over Nick's firm mouth. "You really know how to get to a guy. Everyone in Merivale knows

what my girlfriend is up to—everyone except
me!"

"I had my reasons. You were so swamped
with that paper, I didn't want to add to your
problems."

"Not fair." Nick reached across the counter
and took her hand. "I like knowing what's on
your mind, Lori. Really." The serious look in
his aquamarine eyes emphasized his words.

Happiness welled up inside her as Nick
squeezed Lori's fingers. What a sweet guy! "You
know I'm always honest with you," she told
him, lost in the incredible warmth of his eyes.
"I just thought that I could handle this thing on
my own."

Nick nodded. "Did you find her? Is she
okay?"

"No such luck. We combed the mall, but . . .
no Nora."

"Well, I have some good news. Number
one: I finished my paper early. And number
two: I'm joining Project Pringle, effective immediately."

His smile gave Lori goose bumps as he
casually leaned against the counter. "Where do
you want me to start looking, boss?"

"Oh, Nick, that's great!" Lori's blue eyes
danced with excitement. "Can you check out
the third level? Ann started looking there, but
she didn't have time to check all the shops."

Nick saluted with a dazzling smile. "Will do."

Reaching under the counter, Lori pulled out a walkie-talkie and handed it to Nick. "Give me a call if you find her."

"Very impressive, boss." Eyeing the radio, he moved away as a customer approached the counter. "I'll give it my best shot. Just call me Sherlock Hobart!"

CHAPTER EIGHT

Today is a new day. Anything is possible! Lori reminded herself as she stirred a vat of jalapeño cheese sauce and turned on the steamer. After a few organized searches Nora Pringle was still missing. But maybe today would be Lori's lucky day!

Tio's Tacos was empty, but that would change soon. In an hour or so the lunch crowd would start filing in. And on a Saturday, Merivale Mall was always brimming with shoppers—hungry shoppers.

Lori had just switched on the ice machine when a flash of color caught her eye. It was a purple hat perched on the head of a frail woman in raggedy clothes.

Nora!

"Oh my gosh!" Lori gasped. Her eyes were suddenly riveted to the doorway of Tio's.

Slowly, Nora Pringle made her way across the midway of the mall, her thin arms dragging half a dozen bulging shopping bags.

"She's back! And she seems to be okay!" Lori said, still staring.

"You found your lady?" Isabel looked up from the steamer. "Good for you!"

Lori was so excited and relieved, she wasn't sure what to do first. She wanted to tell Nora about the social service agency. She wanted to ask the woman about employment possibilities, living quarters, relatives and friends.

"First things first." Eyes lit with determination, Lori stuffed three tacos into a bag and scooted around the counter. "Put these on my tab," she told Isabel. "I'll be right back."

"Good luck," the cook called after her.

Blood pounding in her ears, Lori rushed out through the doorway of Tio's and scanned the first level of Merivale Mall. She found Nora Pringle huddled on a bench, crouched over a notepad.

Take it easy! Lori told herself, not wanting to frighten Miss Pringle away. Quietly, cautiously, she approached the frail woman.

"Miss Pringle?" Lori was so nervous, her voice came out in a tiny squeak.

The woman looked up from her frantic scribblings. Fear and suspicion darkened her eyes as she examined Lori.

"Miss Pringle, I'm Lori Randall." She smiled, giving Nora a moment to warm up to her.

Still dubious, Nora stood up, as if ready to flee.

Lori forged ahead, "I, um, I work at Tio's Tacos, and I . . . have some free samples for you."

Suddenly, her mother's words flashed through Lori's mind. *Sometimes homeless people are too proud to accept charity.* Well, she would have to make this sound like a special offer instead.

"Tio's Tacos," she repeated. "We're giving out free tacos . . . as part of a new advertising campaign." She held the paper bag out to Nora. "Hope you enjoy them!" Lori said with a sunny smile.

Clutching her notebook to her chest, Nora stared at the bag of tacos and shook her head. "No, thank you, dear. I'm not hungry."

Not hungry? Lori was stunned. The gaunt hollows in Nora's cheeks belied her words. "Well, these are free samples. Why don't you take them anyway? For when you're hungry . . . later?"

"No, young lady." In a few quick moves Nora gathered her possessions and started scuttling away. "Thank you anyway," she called as she beat a hasty retreat toward the escalator.

Lori was left holding the bag of food. Her

pretty pink mouth hung open in shock and her heart was heavy with disappointment. Nora Pringle had turned down her first gesture of assistance.

The scent of corn meal filled the air as Lori rested the bag of tacos in the crook of her arm. How could Nora turn them down? Of course, Tio's Tacos weren't gourmet cuisine, but they could make a decent meal.

If Miss Pringle was too proud to accept food, she could starve! How in the world would Lori ever get through to the poor woman?

Of all the nerve!

Her perfect white teeth were tightly clenched as Danielle stared out the huge window of the Sharp mansion. The sun had set. The sky was a glow of crimson and lavender beyond the sculptured hedges of the front yard. Another Saturday night—and no Don!

Where was he? How could he do this to her—again? One thing was for sure: Don James wasn't going to stand her up twice in a row and live to tell the tale!

As she paced across the plush living room carpet, Danielle considered her options. She'd already called the James's house, but there was no answer. She'd even phoned the garage where Don worked. The grease monkey there explained that Don had taken the entire day off.

So she'd waited, nearly wearing a trail in

the expensive carpet while the minutes ticked off on her mother's elegant Swiss clock.

Five o'clock, five-thirty. Six, six-thirty! In a minute Danielle was going to start chewing the glossy polish off her manicured nails!

The drone of a motorcycle engine added fuel to her fiery temper. So . . . the king of cool had finally arrived. Too late! At this point they would never make it to Philadelphia on time.

Steaming, Danielle threw open the door before Don even had a chance to ring the doorbell.

Fists clenched and ready for battle, she lashed out at him. "Don't even tell me—let me guess. You got a flat tire and had to melt down rubber bands to make a replacement. No, wait, that's too unusual. Your dog ate your homework. Is that it? Or maybe you were hijacked to China and had to dig your way back!"

Hands on her hips, she lowered her voice to a menacing tone. "I know you must have an incredible, whopping excuse for completely ruining our trip to Philadelphia!"

Flexing his fingers around the handlebars of his bike, Don leaned back and whistled. "Easy, Red. You're liable to blow a gasket." He slung a jean-clad leg over the back of the motorcycle and sauntered up the front steps. "I'm sorry about the concert."

His apology seemed genuine, but Danielle's temper was too far gone. "*Sorry* just isn't good enough. *Sorry* won't get me into a Bad Boys concert. What happened to you? What could possibly be more important than a concert in the city?"

With a calculating look in his dark eyes, Don studied her for a moment. "Do you really want to know?" he asked. "Would you like to see what distracted me?"

No! I want to cry and kick and scream and throw a tantrum! Danielle's green eyes were still ablaze with fury.

But deep inside she knew it would be useless to totally lose it. If she blew up, Don would go away, and she'd be left to spend Saturday night alone in this tomblike house.

Raking her hair away from her face in a pouting gesture, she sighed, "Oh, all right. Show me." *Show me your excuse for shattering my dreams of a perfect date!*

Although Danielle's temper was still simmering when she pulled Don's extra helmet over her thick, coppery-red hair, she began to cool down.

As she rode on the back of Don's bike, buffeted by fragrant evening breezes, she felt glad just to be near him. Leaning against his broad back, with her arms wrapped tightly around his lean waist, Danielle began to wonder if her feelings for this guy were rocketing out of control.

Her heart sank when they pulled up in front of the James's house.

"Here!" she snapped. "You skipped a concert just so you could bring me back here?"

Don laughed. "It's safe, Red. I promise. My parents are out for the evening."

Inside the house Don led her down to the basement, where a workroom was set up. Expecting to see a car engine or a carpentry bench, Danielle was baffled by the sight of a large camera.

"You've been taping a video?" she asked.

"Nope. A movie. Sixteen millimeter." Don's eyes gleamed as he hoisted the camera to his shoulder. "This baby's my pride and joy. It's got most of the features the pros use. I've been shooting in black and white, since the developing is cheaper that way. But I like the contrasts too. Look in here . . ."

As Danielle put her eye up to the camera lens, he helped her focus on the basement window.

"It's . . . it's interesting," she murmured, "but—"

"And then, after we shoot the footage, I use this baby to put it all together." He showed her his editing bench, set up to screen and splice individual frames of the film.

"Not too shabby, huh, Red?" His voice swelled with pride. "Took me a while to save up for this equipment. And I had to buy it secondhand, but it all works. Shoots some mean angles. We've been filming for a couple of weeks, but tonight I kind of got carried away editing.''

"I'll bet." Danielle was stunned. A movie? Don? She had never realized he had any interest in the artistic side of life.

And yet, as she held the camera against her shoulder and worked the zoom lens, she remembered their very first date—how Don was mesmerized by a foreign film.

Back then Danielle had been embarrassed by her feelings for Don. Oh, she'd been crazy about him personally, but socially she knew he was the kiss of death. She'd lived in fear that her friends would find out she was dating a loser from a motorcycle gang.

To avoid a confrontation with her friends, she had dragged Don to an artsy cinema on the far side of town. She didn't really pay much attention to the movie that was playing there—a foreign film with subtitles. But Don had been spellbound.

Don James, film maker. A thrill ran through her as the idea began to sink in. Her boyfriend was artistic, maybe even destined for stardom . . . Hollywood . . . glitter and glitz!

All thoughts of the missed concert flew from Danielle's mind as new possibilities bloomed. Handing the camera back to Don, she flashed him one of her dazzling smiles.

"So how about a sneak preview?" she suggested. "Can I see the movie you're working on?"

Don hesitated. "The editing is still kind of rough," he said, lowering the camera into its tripod.

"Pretty please?" Danielle batted her thick eyelashes, sure that the stunning gesture would win him over.

"Well, just remember that it needs some work," he said, threading a ribbon of film through the projector. "Have a seat."

Settling onto the corner of a worn chintz sofa, Danielle could barely contain her curiosity. *Don't be too critical!* she reminded herself, prepared for a cheesy, amateur production.

A moment later the lights went out, and Don focused the projection on a blank area of the basement wall.

Danielle smiled as she recognized the actors. All the parts were played by Don's former housemates—Zack and the other guys Danielle had seen hanging out at the Video Arcade.

But as the gripping story unfolded, Danielle saw beyond the familiar faces, beyond the familiar setting of Merivale. It was as if a secret window of her mind had been discovered and thrown open to the world.

The film was about a boy who was challenged to a motorcycle race. The opening scenes had an air of menace and doom, created by quick cuts and unusual camera angles.

Poised on the edge of her seat, Danielle watched as the race began. The tension was so heavy and thick, it made her heart pound, thundering in her ears.

The boy's bike veered out of control, heading for a stony cliff—and certain death.

Danielle gasped as gravel flew out behind the tires.

But then the kid skidded away from the crumbling edge of the cliff, and the bike glided back onto the pavement. He didn't crash—and he won the race!

The ending had an interesting twist. After he won the race, the guy kept on going, riding faster and faster, farther and farther, flying down the highway on to a new life.

Although the film was only fifteen minutes long and there was no sound, it was a masterpiece. Still riveted to her seat, Danielle felt shaky and breathless and genuinely moved.

Swiping at the tears in her eyes, she took a deep breath as Don flicked on the lights. "It's wonderful," she whispered. Her heart was bursting with pride and enthusiasm. She leapt to her feet, ran to Don, and gave him a jubilant hug. "In fact, I think it's a masterpiece!"

Obviously relieved that she liked it, Don held her close for a moment, savoring her praise. "Thanks, Red." He loosened his grip so that he could stare into her eyes. "I guess that means you like it. . . ."

"*Like* it?" Slipping out of his arms, Danielle put her fists on her hips in a determined stance. "I *love* it! You're really talented, Don. How long have you been working on this?"

Don grinned. "Not too long. But I've always dreamed of making films. Used to stay up all night watching old movies on TV."

Danielle watched as he took the reel off the projector and cradled it in his hands. She could tell that film making was more than just a hobby to him. He really cared about this movie.

"You know," he confessed, "I used to daydream about getting out of this dump and attending film school at U.C.L.A. That's where a lot of the pros got their training. It would be—I don't know—kind of like the ultimate dream come true."

The glimmer in his dark eyes died as Don put the reel back into its case. "But . . . you know how things go. That could never happen."

"Why not?" Danielle asked. "Why shouldn't it happen? With talent like yours, you can do anything you want." When he shook his head, she persisted. "Don, you can write your own ticket to Hollywood!"

There was a bitter edge to his laughter. "Get real, Red. First of all, I don't have the bucks for a famous school like that. Besides, U.C.L.A. would never let me in. Not with my lousy grades."

"You can't let that stop you!" Wheels started

spinning in Danielle's head, reeling off new possibilities. There was a way around any obstacle—and she'd had loads of experience with figuring out the angles.

"A recommendation from a big-name director would help, wouldn't it?" Her emerald eyes sparkled deviously. "U.C.L.A. would manage to overlook your grades if you had a letter from some hotshot. Right?"

"That's true."

"Sooo . . . why don't you get a recommendation?"

Don shook his head. "I don't have any connections in the film indus—"

"But you can get them," Danielle interrupted. She tapped one long, manicured fingernail against the metal film canister. "This movie is your ticket to success. Any director would be a fool not to recognize the creative talent behind your film."

A satisfied smile lit Danielle's face as all the pieces of her latest scheme fell into place. "Finish your editing, make a copy of the film, then send it to a director you admire."

She settled on Don's editing bench and crossed her slender legs. "After a director sees this flick, he'll be putty in your hands."

Thoughtfully, Don looked down at the film canister in his hands. "There is one director— George Colby. His work is dynamite. And the guy has a reputation for helping young film makers get their start. He even set up the Colby Foundation to assign grants to students."

"So what are you waiting for?" Danielle demanded. "It sounds absolutely perfect!"

Don's smile was so hopeful, so eager, it warmed Danielle right down to her toes.

"It's worth a shot, I guess." He shrugged. "You never know."

"Exactly."

Putting the canister aside, Don moved behind Danielle and dropped his hands onto her shoulders. The warmth of his palms seemed to singe her skin, even through her cashmere sweater.

"You know, you're pretty good at giving advice, Red. Beauty and brains too. You're a lethal combination."

I hope so! Danielle thought. As soon as she got Don's film career on track, she was going to concentrate her lethal powers on romance—with a capital R!

As Don's hands gripped her slender shoulders, she thought she'd melt under his touch. He was standing so close, she knew he'd kiss her as soon as she turned around. Butterflies swirled through her. Don could be so romantic when he wasn't preoccupied with problems.

And they had problems galore. She was sick and tired of making up stories to tell Teresa and Heather. And she was bored with the role of dutiful girlfriend. Of course, she was still crazy about Don . . . maybe even falling in love with him.

But it was time to settle these little problems once and for all so that Don could focus his attention on her favorite subject—the irresistible Danielle Sharp!

CHAPTER NINE

"Okay, Danielle. Spill the beans," Teresa demanded.

"She *has* been awfully subdued, hasn't she?" Heather's blue gaze raked over Danielle in search of incriminating evidence.

Danielle was grateful for the dim lighting of L'Argent, the posh restaurant on the top level of Merivale Mall. In the flickering candle-light maybe her friends wouldn't recognize the deceptive mannerisms of a liar.

"Don't be silly," Danielle said, faking a yawn. "I'm just a little drained after such a wild weekend." She rolled her green eyes dreamily.

"You do have a few shadows under your eyes," Heather agreed.

That's impossible! Danielle bristled at her friend's comment. Her face was made up to sheer perfection! But she kept her snide answer to herself, not wanting to be on the defensive already.

"So how was the concert?" Teresa probed. "Who drove to Philadelphia?"

"Don, of course," Danielle answered. "But we took my car."

Heather and Teresa exchanged curious glances.

"Oh, really?" Heather asked.

"Yes, really," Danielle snapped.

"That's funny," Teresa said. "My mother swore she saw your BMW parked in front of your house on Saturday night when she dropped by to—"

"Well, she must have been mistaken," Danielle insisted, snatching up the linen napkin on the table in front of her and shaking out the accordion pleats. "We got there a little late . . . but the concert was terrific."

More enthusiasm! She kicked herself under the table. Her friends would never buy this story if she didn't tell it with a feverish pitch.

"The concert hall was packed with people. The fans were like . . . like a mob of crazed animals," Danielle continued.

What was she saying? The Bad Boys weren't a hard rock band! Their fans were usually carefree and mellow. A quick glance at her friends told her that they didn't notice. She was safe—for now.

"It's too bad about the lead guitarist." Heather stabbed a slice of turkey from her chef's salad and popped it into her mouth.

"Really," Teresa agreed. "Could you see the accident from your seats?"

Danielle nearly choked on a lettuce leaf. *Accident? The lead guitarist?* What were they talking about? Stalling for time, she coughed and reached for her crystal water goblet.

"Was it horrible?" Heather persisted.

Still not sure what they were referring to, Danielle nodded. "Yes . . . terrible."

"The write-up in the newspaper made it sound like a big deal, but you can never tell about that sort of thing." Heather's slate-blue eyes pierced Danielle to the bone. "Did it ice your dream date?"

"No . . . of course not." A black cloud of dread invaded Danielle's heart. Obviously, something had happened at the concert—something unusual. Her friends knew more about it than she did, and she was supposed to have been there!

She was trapped—cornered! But now that she'd begun to spin a wild tale, she had no choice but to continue.

"To tell you the truth, nothing could have ruined my date with Don." A dreamy, faraway look softened Danielle's face as she rambled on.

"I think the most romantic moment was when they played *Stardust Dreams*. Don's strong arms were wrapped around me, holding me close. And then, at the end of the song, he kissed me."

Danielle's eyes closed as she wallowed in her crafty lie. *Let them mull that one over!* Nearly purring with satisfaction, she opened her eyes and daintily pushed away her plate.

But instead of envy, her story had inspired cold suspicion.

"*Stardust Dreams*?" Teresa echoed. "The papers said the Bad Boys never got to play the song, since the lead guitarist sprained his ankle and had to leave the stage. They couldn't possibly play *Stardust Dreams* without Johnny Dean on lead guitar!"

So that was what had happened! Danielle nibbled on her lower lip, trying to keep her cool while she thought up a quick explanation.

"Isn't that odd," Heather said. "Maybe you and Don went to the wrong concert."

"Or maybe they didn't go to the Bad Boys concert at all." Teresa's voice was razor-sharp. "Your story doesn't hold water, Danielle. Why don't you tell us what *really* happened?"

Heather joined the attack. "What's the matter, Danielle? Are you embarrassed that your dream boy stood you up?"

"No, I—"

"Or maybe your romance with Don James isn't all it's cracked up to be," Teresa interrupted.

Danielle glared at her friends. "I'm sure you wouldn't understand," she said, seething. "You two wouldn't recognize a heavy romance if it fell from the sky and knocked you out cold."

Teresa gasped, recoiling in anger.

Only Heather remained cool. "No need to get nasty, Danielle. We're just stating the facts." She leaned forward, whispering in a confidential tone, "Sometimes the truth hurts, though. Doesn't it?"

The comment was like a knife jabbing Danielle's heart. Heather didn't realize how right she was. Danielle's romance with Don was loaded with sizzling heat. It just wasn't the kind of thing Danielle could boast about.

Her friends would never understand why she'd missed the concert. They'd laugh if they knew she'd spent Saturday night watching a homemade movie in Don's basement.

It was so unfair! If Don cared about her, he should show it in ways her friends could see. Where were the flowers, candy, music, and moonlight? Don was forgetting all the little perks a girl like Danielle deserved!

She would have to talk to him, take him by the hand and lead him down the primrose path of romance. Danielle had high hopes for Don

James. Once he was wrapped around her little finger, he would give her everything she wanted.

In the meantime she needed to talk her way out of this ugly little scene—and save face with her friends.

Chewing on a bread stick, she studied their faces. They reminded her of vultures, circling and swooping low, waiting for a kill. Teresa's lips were pursed under her freckled upturned nose, and Heather's cool, probing gaze belied her placid smile.

Sometimes Danielle wondered why she hung out with these snobby girls. They had a competitive streak that allowed no mercy.

On the other hand, Heather and Teresa were the two most popular, most envied girls at the exclusive Atwood Academy. When it came to money, class, and beauty, Danielle couldn't deny that she belonged among their ranks.

Although Danielle was sick and tired of acting out this little charade, this would be her final performance. After tonight her romance with Don would be the envy of every girl in Merivale. Instead of doubting her, Heather and Teresa would be rushing to her side for advice about *their* boyfriends.

After she and Don made a splash at the Overlook tonight, Danielle's friends would eat their words.

"If it's proof you want, it's proof you'll get," Danielle announced. "Although I don't know why you two are so skeptical. It couldn't be that you're just a teensy-weensy bit jealous," she needled them. "Could it?"

"From what I've seen, there's nothing to be jealous of," Teresa snapped with a lift of her freckled nose.

The waiter came and offered them dessert and coffee. When the girls declined, he tallied up their check and placed it on the table—right in front of Teresa!

Danielle's hand flew to her face to cover a nasty smirk. Since the girls dined at L'Argent on a regular basis, they played a little game with the tab. The entire bill was always paid by the girl the waiter handed it to.

Tonight Teresa was the loser! Danielle was tickled that her snooty friend had lost the game, even if none of the girls would have a problem paying the bill. Teresa and Heather had unlimited allowances.

"Well . . ." Standing, Danielle folded her napkin and dropped it onto the table. "I really should get going. The Overlook is so romantic on a clear night like tonight. Don and I just can't bear to miss a minute of it."

"The Overlook?" Heather's eyebrows rose at the mention of Merivale's popular lover's lane. "Sounds a bit hot and heavy for a girl with a fictitious boyfriend."

"That's true," Danielle replied. "So I won't expect to see *you two* there." She slipped her suede bag over her shoulder and fluffed her coppery hair.

"Thanks for the dinner," she told Teresa. *And thanks loads for the friendly advice!*

When Danielle strode through the lower level of Merivale Mall on her way out, Lori was still handling the dinner rush at Tio's.

Although there were at least half a dozen people waiting in line for service, Lori's mind was elsewhere. She moved mechanically, pouring sodas, sprinkling cheese on beef enchiladas, smiling cheerfully at each customer.

But all the while her thoughts were haunted by Nora Pringle.

How could the woman survive without some help? Lori had to tell her about the social service agency. But how would she ever get close to Nora? The poor woman seemed so shy and frightened of contact.

The dinner rush was still going strong when Lori noticed the object of her thoughts. Decked out in her unmistakable purple beret and raggedy clothes, Nora Pringle slowly passed by the entrance of Tio's.

The sight of the feeble woman made Lori sigh. She couldn't leave the counter now, not with four hungry people standing in line.

She fought back a feeling of helplessness. There had to be something she could do for

Nora! She wasn't rich, but she was determined. Didn't she have something special to offer?

A moment later an idea popped into Lori's head. She was a practiced seamstress, and Nora Pringle needed clothes. Lori could start with some of her mother's discarded garments, bring them up-to-date, and scale them down to Nora's size!

As Lori's idea gained momentum, she began to feel hopeful again. Miss Pringle would be transformed by Lori's fashions!

And then, once the ice was broken, Lori could use the opportunity to tell her about Mimi Turner's agency.

Bursting with new enthusiasm, Lori handed a customer a tray of food. "Thank you, sir, and please come again!" she said with a sunny grin.

Winking, the man picked up the tray. "Now I know what they mean by service with a smile!"

CHAPTER TEN

Nothing was going right today!

Leaning back in her seat, Danielle sighed and stared up through the open sunroof of her car. The inky black sky was studded with a handful of winking stars. The Overlook was known for its heavenly views. But, at the moment, Danielle felt uninspired.

At last, she and Don had made it to Merivale's hottest spot for a romantic date. Danielle had been eager to spring her latest scheme . . . until she noticed Don's sullen mood.

Arms crossed, eyes staring straight ahead, Don looked like a condemned criminal awaiting execution.

Oh, no! Not again! Danielle knew Don had a

few things to straighten out in his life, but this was getting ridiculous! When would he forget about his problems and concentrate on her?

"Do you want to talk about it?" she asked, gritting her teeth to play the role of dutiful girlfriend one last time.

Rubbing his eyes, Don sighed. "Is it that obvious?"

When she nodded, he explained. "It's just another battle at home. My mother took a second job to make some extra money, and my dad's furious. I just happened to walk into the crossfire. Now they're convinced that it's all my fault. Their expenses are higher now that I've been living with them."

"But that's not your fault. How can they blame you?"

Don shrugged. "Who knows? Nothing I do is right for them. They get ticked off when I hang around the house, but they don't want me going out either."

"But you're seventeen years old!" Danielle protested. "Why do they treat you like a preschooler?"

"Who knows why parents act so strange. They've lost control of their lives, so they blame me. I'm the only person they can control—or so they think. Sometimes I'm tempted to rev up my bike and ride off. Take Route 32 to the interstate, and just keep on rolling."

"Now, *that* sounds exciting. But you'd have to take me with you," Danielle teased.

"Sure, Red. Just you and me, cruising off to a better place, a better life."

"Just like the kid in your film," Danielle pointed out.

Don's black eyes glimmered. "Exactly." As if he were concentrating on the dream, his hands gripped the leather-wrapped steering wheel of Danielle's BMW.

"You know," he continued, "I jumped on your suggestion about the movie. I had to make a few phone calls out to California, but eventually I got the address of the studio where George Colby shoots his films. I'm sending him a copy of my film tomorrow."

"That's great! I'll keep my fingers crossed for you."

Don's smile reminded Danielle why she bothered to listen to his problems. She wanted to be near him even if things weren't always perfect. She was really falling for this guy—and hard!

"Listen, Red. If anything happens with my movie, you get ten percent of the deal. Standard agent's cut."

But I want one hundred percent of your heart! A troubled look darkened her green eyes. She knew that Don was going through a rough time, but what about her? She had needs and rights in their relationship too!

Don could tell something was up. His dark eyes narrowed as he scrutinized her. "We've been talking about me all night. I can tell that something's cooking in that beautiful head of yours. What's up?"

It was now or never. Danielle had to either lay her cards on the table or get out of the game. There was no sense in having a quiet, mediocre relationship with Don James. If she wanted a romance with pizzazz, she'd have to go for it.

"It's . . . it's about us." She paused to take a deep breath. "You know how I feel about you, don't you?" she asked, tears glittering in her eyes.

Don reached over and squeezed her hand. "I think so, Red."

"Well . . ." Her voice was low and hoarse. She had planned to pour on the tears to get Don's sympathy, but now her emotions were genuine. This conversation could make or break her relationship with Don.

"I always thought that you cared for me too," she whispered. "But lately I've begun to have my doubts."

Unable to face him, Danielle turned to stare out through the windshield. "I first started having doubts when we missed the trip to Philadelphia. It made me start thinking about all the special things a guy does for a girl he likes. You know . . . little things like flowers and candy."

She paused, hoping Don would agree with her. But the silence stretched on, making Danielle squirm with nervousness.

"I guess it hurts only because . . . because I do like you," she said, beginning to feel awkward.

Why did she have to wear her heart on her sleeve like this? Danielle hated discussing her true feelings. She wanted her life to be perfect, and an admission of hurt was like an admission of failure.

Lifting her hand to his lips, Don kissed the soft skin of her knuckles. "Sorry, Red. You know I'd never do anything to hurt you. At least not intentionally."

When she looked at him, his eyes were dark, his expression serious. He meant every word! Swallowing hard, Danielle fought off the tears that stung the back of her throat. For once in her life she'd found someone who really cared about her.

"To tell you the truth, I didn't realize I was disappointing you." Don reached over to brush a coppery tendril away from her eyes. His hand lingered on her cheek for a moment, then slid down to cup her chin.

His touch sent shivers down her spine. *If only Heather and Teresa could see me now!* she thought, relieved that Don understood her feelings.

"I want to make you happy," he murmured, trailing his fingers around her throat to soothe

the back of her neck. His voice was low. "Jeez, Red. You know I'm crazy about you."

And then he kissed her.

Wrapped in Don's arms, Danielle felt as if she were floating, suspended in the velvety sky along with the stars twinkling above them. She was a diamond, sparkling in the night, the brightest star in the heavens.

She was in love, and Don was crazy about her too.

Lost in Don's kiss, she prayed that it would go on forever and ever.

What a knockout!

Don James watched as Danielle skipped up the porch steps and disappeared through the front door of the Sharp mansion.

He had always had a thing for Danielle Sharp—ever since the sixth grade.

The porch light flickered on and off a few times—her way of saying a final good-night.

Tripping the starter on his motorcycle, Don juiced up the engine and rolled off down the long, circular driveway. As he passed the fancy wrought-iron gate at the foot of the drive, he turned toward the open road, away from home.

He knew it was late. He and Red had spent hours at the Overlook. His mother would be ticked off, but he would deal with her later.

Right now he had some thinking to do. Right now he had to ride.

He hit the back roads in second gear, the wind washing over him, tearing at the sleeves of his cotton shirt. Since the night was so warm, he'd strapped his leather jacket to the back of his bike.

Don James had a lot on his mind. His parents were a royal pain in the neck, and his film demanded a lot of his time. His brain was a wild jumble of thoughts, but *she* topped them all.

Red. Danielle Sharp.

Beautiful, irresistible, clever, slick as ice. Sometimes a little self-centered, but Don knew where she was coming from. You didn't grow up in a mansion on a hill without a few quirks. And Don realized that rich people had their share of problems just like the rest of the world.

He and Danielle had borne their share of problems too. Once she'd made a big deal about his clothes. She wanted him to wear expensive suits like the guys at her fancy school.

Don wanted to make her happy, but he had to be true to himself. He would never dress like a geek—not even for Red.

But things were different now. As Zack would say, he was really losing it. Don was falling for that redheaded rich girl, falling hard and fast.

Sometimes he couldn't believe that Danielle had even given him the time of day. His friends still ribbed him about stepping out of line, dating a rich girl from Wood Hollow Hills, Merivale's poshest neighborhood.

Don didn't have the bucks to compete with the guys she went to school with, but lately Danielle didn't seem to care.

Gravel flew from under the tires as he pulled on the brakes at a stop sign. There were no cars out here at this time of night. Alone in the dark countryside with only the stars above to guide him, Don gunned the engine and rode on.

So what would it take to make Danielle happy? He could play the dating game as well as any other guy. And for the first time in his life, he really wanted to do it.

He would do it for her.

Come tomorrow, Danielle Sharp wouldn't know what hit her.

CHAPTER ELEVEN

"What in the world is that?" Teresa asked, pointing at Danielle's locker.

Danielle's heart stopped dead as she froze midstep in the corridor of Atwood Academy.

"Flowers! They must be for you." Heather grabbed Danielle's arm and dragged her the remaining few feet to get a closer look at the spectacle.

A wicker basket of crimson miniature roses laced with baby's breath hung from the handle of Danielle's locker.

He remembered! Danielle wanted to jump for joy, but she restrained herself and merely flashed her friends a smug smile. Apparently, last night's little chat with Don had done the trick.

"There's a card." Teresa reached into the bouquet of flowers and plucked out a tiny envelope. "What does it say?" she asked, handing it over.

Danielle's emerald eyes flickered with pleasure. Considering Don's laid-back manner, this card was incredibly romantic. "They're from Don, of course," she said, passing the card to Teresa.

"Red roses for a red-haired beauty," Teresa recited, reading Don's message. "Pretty poetic."

"Let me see that!" Still skeptical, Heather snatched the note away. After reading the card herself, she handed it to Danielle and poked a finger at one delicate rosebud. "Well, well, well," she said. "Maybe there's still hope for old Donny-boy."

"Oh, there's more than hope," Danielle insisted, lifting the basket of fragrant flowers to her face and taking a deep breath. "Don't you know what it means when a guy sends red roses? *Red* is the color of *passion!*"

Chocolates—imported from Switzerland!

The package was waiting on the front porch when Danielle got home from school that day. She was so ecstatic, she could barely nibble a morsel of candy.

At last, Don was getting into the swing of things! Before long everyone would know he was the model boyfriend—and their romance would go down in Merivale history.

Without a flicker of hesitation Danielle snatched the box and raced up the stairs to her room. Telephone time!

This scrumptious development had to be reported to Teresa and Heather. Once they got wind of it, everyone in town would know!

Lazily kicking off her shoes, Danielle stretched out on the white leather sofa and pulled the phone into her lap.

Sure-fire celebrity status was just a phone call away. Punching in Heather's number, she smiled. There was at least one advantage to being best friends with the biggest gossips in town!

In a matter of days Merivale's gossip network was abuzz with hot new headlines.

Have you heard about Danielle Sharp and Don James—Merivale's sizzling sensation?

The rumor mills churned with juicy details, hot tips, and wild speculation.

"I think you two are destined to be together—forever!" one sophomore told Danielle while they were waiting in the lunch line at school.

Although Danielle usually ignored little sophomores, she smiled at the girl before paying the cashier.

Atwood Academy's cafeteria was always humming with conversation at lunchtime. And recently, Danielle seemed to be the star of every story. Interested friends stopped by Danielle's table, eager to hear the latest twist in the romantic saga of Merivale's primo sweethearts.

"Your car was spotted at the Overlook last night," said Ashley Shepard.

"That's the third night in a row," Heather added. "Pretty soon you'll be breaking all local records!"

The girls at the table laughed but quickly quieted down when Danielle launched into a tale about last night's date with Don.

Although Danielle loved the attention, she'd discovered that a hot romance could eat up all her free time. She and Don were constantly together, shopping at Merivale Mall, grabbing a bite to eat, going to movies, or stopping at the Overlook to peer at the stars.

And when she wasn't with Don, Danielle was busy feeding Merivale's insatiable appetite for gossip.

By Wednesday night she felt like a high-profile celebrity. Everyone seemed to know who she was and exactly what she was doing every minute of each day.

Staring into the frothy fountain on the first level of Merivale Mall, Danielle considered the price of fame as she waited for Don to show up.

"You must be Danielle Sharp, right?"

Fiery curls swung over Danielle's shoulders as she looked around. The voice belonged to a short, freckled girl with glasses. Now even strange peons felt they had the right to approach her!

Rolling her eyes, Danielle answered, "Yes, that's me."

"Is it true that your boyfriend is taking you out to dinner tonight? At L'Argent?" the girl sputtered.

"What are you—a reporter for the *Merivale Enquirer*?" Danielle snapped. "Lay off!"

With a shrug the short girl backed away and joined her circle of friends. A moment later the girls burst into a fit of giggles as the short girl whispered a report, pointing straight at Danielle.

"Pipsqueak!" Danielle muttered to herself. Now that she had a hot romance going, every punky little kid wanted to know her business.

But it was a small price to pay for popularity. Tonight she and Don were going to have an elegant dinner at L'Argent. Then they'd probably spend the rest of the night stargazing at the Overlook.

Of course, Danielle couldn't stay out too late tonight. Her history teacher was giving a humongous test in the morning, and she hadn't cracked her textbook once this week. But who could concentrate on dusty old history when romance was in the air?

As she looked away from the fountain, a stylish leather jacket caught her eye. Made of worn brown leather, the jacket was decorated with a fringe of red feathers.

Danielle was surprised that the unique western style appealed to her. It was so different from the fashions they were showing at Facades and High Hats this season. But she was even more surprised to discover that the girl wearing the funky jacket was her cousin, Lori Randall.

"Hi, Danielle." Lori's smile was as bright as a sunburst. "How's it going?"

"Fabulous, of course." With a quick glance Danielle made sure none of her snooty friends were in sight. Socializing with a Merivale High kid was totally taboo—even if that kid happened to be your cousin. "I guess you've heard about my latest conquest?"

"Every sizzling word." Even the most elite Atwood gossip eventually made it over to Lori's school. "Congratulations!"

Casually, Danielle threw a lock of hair over one shoulder. "I guess it was always meant to be," she said, taking a closer look at Lori's outfit. For once her cousin wasn't wearing that hideous polyester uniform. "Nice jacket," she said, feeling magnanimous. Thin, beautiful, rich and so much in love, Danielle could afford to be a little gracious.

"Thanks." Lori was particularly proud of this jacket. She'd discovered the beat-up leather shell at a thrift shop, restored it, then added the feather fringe to jazz it up. The result was another exciting Lori Randall creation.

"Speaking of romance, I was just waiting for Mr. Wonderful," Danielle explained.

"And I'm meeting Nick here. Have you seen him around?"

"Not recently." Not long ago, Danielle had set her sights on handsome Nick Hobart. The rivalry between the cousins had been intense for a while. But after the dust had cleared, Nick ended up with Lori—which was fine with Danielle now that her romance with Don was going strong.

"So is it all it's cracked up to be?" Lori teased. "I've heard so many glamorous stories about you and Don, I don't know *what* to believe."

"Believe it!" A smile softened Danielle's pretty face. "I don't know what you've heard, but Don is . . . well, he's a great guy. This could be the real thing, Lori. I mean, I think I'm really falling for him."

"Danielle! That's wonderful!" Delighted, Lori threw her arms around her cousin in a hug. "I'm so happy for you! Isn't love great?"

Pleased by her cousin's reaction, Danielle almost didn't mind that Lori had hugged her smack in the middle of Merivale Mall. Of course, Heather and Teresa would have cringed at the sight, but Danielle's attitude had been softened by the glow of love.

"Oops—there's Nick," Lori said, spotting her boyfriend on the shiny chrome escalator. "Why don't you come on over and say hello?"

"I'd better not." Danielle glanced at her

diamond-studded watch. "Don should be here any minute."

A wise glimmer danced in Lori's pale blue eyes. How unusual to see her cousin eagerly waiting for a guy. In the past Danielle had kept whole flocks of boys waiting at her beck and call.

Maybe the rumors were true. Maybe Danielle was really and truly falling for Don James.

"I can see you've been busy," Nick said as he peeked into the top of the cardboard boxes in his arms. "Is this why I never see you anymore?"

"I'm glad to hear that you missed me." Lori laughed. "But it's only been a few late nights spent at the sewing machine."

A teasing frown settled on Nick's face. "I'm competing with a needle and a one-step button-holer!"

"But you're much better looking!" Hoisting the third box into her arms, Lori closed the trunk of her sporty red Triumph. Although the Spitfire was old, it was her pride and joy. Lori had used her own hard-earned savings to buy the perky little car.

"What next, boss?" A teasing glimmer lit Nick's aquamarine eyes.

"Boss? Gee, I like the sound of that." Lori giggled, pointing across the parking lot. "To the mall!"

As they walked toward the entrance of Merivale Mall, Lori wondered if this plan would work. At least the odds were in her favor. With nearly a dozen revamped dresses to choose from, Nora Pringle had to find something she liked in Lori's collection.

And then Lori would have her chance.

"Where do you want to set this up?" Nick asked, pausing near the glass elevator.

"Let's see . . ." Lori's blue eyes scanned the first level. "Over there, beside that bench." She pointed to a spot between Tio's and Merivale Drugs. Since she had to report to work in an hour, she wanted to leave the clothes in a nearby location.

Placing the boxes of clothes beside the bench, Lori pulled out a hand-lettered sign and propped it against the boxes.

FREE CLOTHES—PLEASE HELP YOURSELF!

"There!" Smiling, she stepped back and surveyed the little display. "That should do it. If Nora sees the sign, maybe she won't feel guilty about taking a few dresses."

Slipping an arm around her shoulders, Nick added, "I hope you're right—for Nora's sake *and* yours."

While Lori staked out the clothes from a nearby bench, Nick went over to The Big Scoop to get ice cream sodas.

After a few minutes two junior-high girls approached the boxes.

They're not for you! Lori wanted to shout. Instead, she watched silently as the girls sorted through the clothes, unfolding a few dresses and holding them up to each other.

Finally they moved on—without taking anything.

"Kind of pretty, but too old-fashioned for me." Lori heard one girl remark.

Good! Lori thought. The clothes would be perfect for Nora.

A few minutes later Lori couldn't believe her good luck. Miss Pringle was ambling across the midway, headed smack in the direction of the clothes!

Heart pounding with excitement, Lori jumped to her feet and stuffed her shaky hands into the pockets of her jacket. Reminding herself to be patient, she watched and waited.

When Nora Pringle spotted the sign, she paused. Lori smiled as Nora eased her shopping bags to the floor and peered cautiously, almost curiously, at the boxes of clothes.

Sure of Nora's interest, Lori was just about to take a step forward when Nora picked up her belongings and moved on—without taking a stitch of the clothing!

"Wait! Don't go away empty-handed!" Lori called, frustrated.

But Miss Pringle was already too far away to hear her.

Disappointment swept through Lori as she

walked over to the boxes and picked up the sign.

Why didn't it work?

She picked up a navy blue dress, an old frock of her mother's that she'd turned into a simple, straight-cut jersey. Fingering the smooth wool, she fought off a twinge of regret. She'd worked so hard on these clothes, staying up late at night, getting up extra early in the morning.

But her plan had failed.

Although Lori wasn't a quitter, she had to admit she'd met her match in Nora Pringle. If the woman didn't want help, Lori could hardly force her to accept it.

"What happened?" Nick's eyes were wide with concern.

As always, sparks flew when their eyes met. *Be grateful for all the wonderful things in your own life*, Lori reminded herself. *Be happy that you're standing here beside Nick Hobart—and he's holding a delicious ice cream soda!*

"Did you talk to Nora?" he asked.

"No." Lori sighed, dropping the navy dress back into its box. "I guess I've got to admit that Nora Pringle is way, way out of my league."

CHAPTER TWELVE

How can they yell so early in the morning?

Danielle's eyes were barely open, only partially rimmed with eyeliner, when the angry voices rang through the house. Her parents were arguing again.

I wonder if they're talking about me? With forest-green eye pencil in hand, she tiptoed out to the hall to tune in on their heated conversation.

"I'm sick of it, Michael," her mother shouted. "Sick and tired of living in this one-horse town in the middle of nowhere! Why don't we move to the city, where the . . ."

Same old song. Danielle's mother had wanted to move away from Merivale for years.

"We can't just pick up and leave this town!"

Mike Sharp retorted. "My entire business is here! All my contacts, my associates . . ."

And that's a familiar line.

Grateful that she wasn't the object of their fury, Danielle slipped back into her bedroom to finish dressing for school.

She sat on the bed and pulled on a pair of soft red suede boots, folding them over the bottom of her blue jeans. Then, with a wide yawn, she fell back on the bed and closed her eyes for two more precious minutes of rest.

Despite its varied delights, romance could be exhausting. Last night she and Don had appeared at the Overlook for the fifth night in a row, breaking a local record!

But her legendary love life had required a few sacrifices. Danielle had totally botched her history test, forgotten about an English paper that was due the next day, and flubbed up a French essay. She never had time for her friends anymore. Don took up every moment, every hour, every single day.

And yet she couldn't complain. She'd gotten exactly what she'd wanted. Romance had its price, but love was super wonderful!

The shrill voices downstairs roused her again. Maybe she could sneak out the front door without being heard. Danielle was hungry, but who wanted to eat breakfast when it was being served in a war zone?

*   *   *

"Are you Danielle Sharp?"

Danielle's delicate jaw clenched at the sound of the strange voice. Now that she was a celebrity, she didn't have a moment's peace—not at the mall, not at Atwood.

Stuffing a textbook into her locker, she slammed the door closed, then turned to face the intruder.

"Who wants to know?" she asked, scowling at the tall, thin girl dressed in a freshman gym uniform.

A red blush crept up the girl's face as she stared down at the ground. "Your boyfriend," she mumbled.

"What did you say?" Danielle rested her hands on her hips. "Speak up."

The freshmen girl shyly handed her a crumpled note. "He's waiting outside, behind the field house. Ms. Malone almost chased him away . . . but he talked her out of it."

Danielle opened the wrinkled note.

Red—
Let's ride off into the sunset.
　　　　　—D.

Bad timing. Danielle frowned as she thought about the English paper she had to get started on. She couldn't afford to miss history, and her French vocabulary was taking a beating.

But Don was waiting.

And, on a gorgeous day like today, how could she resist?

"I knew you'd come." Don's easy smile tugged at Danielle's heart. "No girl can resist a ride on a mean machine like this."

"Don't push your luck," Danielle teased, pulling on a helmet and climbing onto the back of Don's motorcycle.

Although Danielle had lived in Merivale all her life, she'd never really explored the surrounding countryside. As Don's bike roared toward the mountains, Danielle's heart raced with excitement. The wind touseled the ends of her hair and billowed over the sleeves of her linen blouse, reminding her that she was young and alive and free.

When Don turned off the main highway, they plunged into the dark shade of towering evergreen trees. The air was filled with scents of honeysuckle, wild roses, wet earth, and pine, all mingling together in a fragrance even sweeter than Fallen Angel.

"Hold on tight, Red," Don called back to her. "It gets rocky up ahead."

Leaning against him, she wrapped her arms firmly around his lean waist. *Close enough to feel his heartbeat.* Danielle closed her eyes and surrendered to the magic of the moment. *Heaven!* she thought. *I must be in heaven.*

They rode for a while, slicing through the

cool mountain air, occasionally passing fields of grazing horses and cows.

Danielle had always loved Don's wild, reckless streak. But now, riding the open road with him, she began to understand his craving for freedom. There was power in the open road— power, energy, and hope. A fabulous new world lingered just over the next hill, just around the next corner.

A few miles down the road they came to a wide clearing. Don rolled the bike into the shade of an oak tree, then shoved the kickstand down with the heel of his boot.

"End of the line, lady."

Danielle jumped off the bike and tugged off her helmet. Looking around, she had to admit that this was a beautiful spot. She'd always preferred the slick excitement of the city to the boring old boondocks, but then again, she'd never been alone in the woods with Don James.

"So what do we do now?" she asked.

"Eat." Don pulled off his helmet and slung it over the handlebars.

"Eat what? Are we going to scavenge for wild roots and berries? Go bear hunting? Fishing?" Danielle hoped not. She wasn't in the mood to get her nails dirty.

"Nah." Don removed a bag from the pouch on his bike. "Too much work. I brought some sandwiches."

A path through the trees led them to a grassy hill overlooking a crystal-clear pond.

Don spread a blanket in the grass while Danielle took inventory on lunch.

"Sandwiches, sodas, fruit, pretzels . . ." Her emerald eyes sparkled with amusement. "Not bad for a spur-of-the-moment escape to the mountains."

"I never ride off into the sunset without rations," Don explained.

While they ate they watched as a family of ducks splashed in the pond below. Don gave her the latest update on his parents—definitely bad news. But he also mentioned that he'd mailed his film off to George Colby.

"You know," he said, "one of these days my dad will be watching television, glued to the screen, and one of my films will come on."

Don laughed. "I'd love to see his face when my name flashes by in the credits. He always tells me I'm a total zero." Don's dark gaze met her eyes. "I can't wait to show him he's wrong."

"And you will," Danielle assured him, her eyes wide with understanding. "I know how it feels to be invisible at home. You've just got to live your own life and forget about your parents."

Taking her hand, Don pulled her down on the blanket.

"You know, Red, for a poor little rich girl, you understand an awful lot about a guy's problems."

Danielle closed her eyes. The sun felt so warm on her face, she wanted to melt away and sink into the field of clover behind them.

"Well . . ." She took a deep breath of pine-scented air. "I guess I understand what you're going through because—because I have problems with my parents too."

"Somehow that doesn't surprise me."

Opening one eye, Danielle gave him a suspicious look. "Is it that obvious?"

"Not at all. Everyone in Merivale thinks your life is perfect." He squeezed her hand. "Well, almost everyone. I've always been a pretty decent judge of character. I could tell that your mother was unhappy the first day I met her."

"Unhappy is putting it mildly. She's miserable—and she does her best to make everyone else in the family miserable too. Sometimes I'd give anything just to get away from them."

Painful remnants of the morning's battle stabbed at Danielle's heart, making her throat tighten with tension. She started to tell Don about the breakfast war, and then one thing led to another.

Soon stories and sorrows and tears were spilling forth, tumbling out before she could stop them. She told things she'd never shared with anyone else in the world. She told him about all the hurt, all the pain she'd suffered listening to their constant arguments, sometimes getting caught in the middle, sometimes being completely ignored.

Her throat became thick with tears, but still she continued. "I know they want the best for me. But an expensive car and designer clothes aren't enough. I wish I had a family—with parents who got along and loved each other."

Danielle sniffed back a tear. "Sure it's nice to have money and nice things. But I'd . . . I'd rather have parents who really cared about me." Her voice broke in a tiny sob.

"I know," Don said, gently wiping the tears from her smooth cheeks. Slipping his arms around her shoulders, he rocked her soothingly. "I know exactly how it feels."

He held her while she cried, rocking her in his arms, waiting patiently until her sobs eased.

Wrapped in Don's arms, Danielle felt cushioned and protected. Instead of being embarrassed by her tears, she felt relieved, as if they'd washed away years of heartache.

Rubbing her eyes, she laughed. "I must look like a wreck."

"You look gorgeous, Red."

"You know, I've never told anyone about my parents. Somehow I just knew you would understand."

"And I do."

The smoky look in his eyes told her it was true. Don understood her—maybe better than she understood herself.

Suddenly Danielle wanted to tell him everything. For the first time in her life she was falling in love—deeply, truly in love.

A brisk breeze blew over them, making Danielle shiver. Her skin was tingling, either from the wind or from the look in Don's eyes.

Should I tell him? Does he love me too?

The answer was in his eyes. Her heart thundered in her ears as she realized he was going to kiss her.

Cupping her chin, he lifted her face to his in a kiss Danielle would never, ever forget.

They spent the afternoon walking along the lake, talking more about rocky times at home.

Warmed by the sun, they sat on the edge of a gray, weathered dock, pulled off their boots, and dipped their feet in the icy pond.

"Go for a swim?" Don asked.

"Not on your life." Danielle kicked her feet in the water, spraying Don with a few drops. "There are icebergs out there!"

They also spent a lazy hour stretched out in a clover field, searching for four-leaf clovers.

"Here's one with six leaves." Don plucked it from a patch of green weeds. "Does that count?"

"No," Danielle insisted. "It's got to be four."

"What if we pull off two leaves?"

"Cheater!" she cried, tossing a clump of clover in his direction.

Before the afternoon ended, Danielle found her lucky clover leaf. With great care she picked it and tucked it into the pocket of her jeans.

"What are you going to wish for, Red?"

A sultry smile settled on Danielle's face. "If I tell you, it won't come true," she murmured, then added, "but you probably know anyway."

Don stared at her for a long, silent moment. "I probably do."

When the sun began to set, they headed for home. The western sky was like an artist's palette colored with swirls of blue, purple, red, and orange paints. Frowning, Danielle tightened her grip around Don's waist.

Although they were headed toward Merivale, she felt as if they were going in the wrong direction. Why were they headed back to the source of all their problems?

Thinking of the clover in her pocket, she closed her eyes and made the most romantic wish she could imagine. She wanted to ride off into the sunset with Don . . . and never, ever have to turn back.

CHAPTER THIRTEEN

"Excuse me, miss."

The stranger's voice brought Lori back to earth. Staring at a snowy display in the window of Benson's, she'd been daydreaming about knitting bulky sweaters with colorful designs.

"Sorry to bother you." The voice belonged to a teenager with wild brunette curls. "I don't mean to be nosy, but I was wondering where you got that sweater. It's exactly what I've been looking for, but I haven't seen it in any of the shops here."

A pleased smile curved her lips as Lori looked down at the creamy white sweater with tiny blue and metallic gold leaves embroidered along the neckline.

"You won't find a top like this in Merivale Mall," Lori said. "The sweater used to belong to my mom, and I added the embroidery myself."

"You must be kidding! It looks so . . . professional." The teenager seemed impressed but also determined. "Do you take orders?" she persisted. "I'd love to have one. I'll pay you." Her dark eyes narrowed, assessing Lori from head to toe. "We look about the same size. And I adore those colors. I'll even take that one."

For the third time that day Lori was flabbergasted. "I'm afraid it's not for sale." An offer like this was high praise for her designing skills. She was tickled by the flattery—but she could hardly sell the clothes off her back!

"But it's perfect for me," the girl insisted.

Fingering the fine embroidery on one sleeve, Lori explained, "Sewing is just a hobby of mine. I haven't made too many outfits for other people yet."

"But you *should*!" the girl raved. "You'd make a fortune! Look, why don't I give you my number, just in case you ever decide to branch out." Dark curls fell into her eyes as she rooted through her purse for pen and paper.

I must be doing something right! Lori thought as she waited for the girl to scribble down her phone number. Two other people had approached Lori earlier to inquire about her bleached denim miniskirt and her fringed leather jacket, which she now carried slung over one shoulder. All three of the strangers had admired her clothes, asking where she'd bought them.

Three times is the charm! she thought with a smile. Now if someone complimented her on her white canvas tennies, she could direct them straight to the sales rack at Shoe Hut!

"Give me a call if you change your mind." With a toss of her dark curls the teen handed the slip of paper to Lori. "I'd love to own some original fashions!"

"I'll let you know," Lori promised, tucking the note into her purse and turning back to study the wintry window display once again.

But as she stared into the plate-glass window, she noticed another reflection standing behind her.

It was Nora Pringle!

Lingering just a few feet away, Nora had witnessed the entire conversation. The woman's beady eyes now followed the teenager whose dark curls bounced as she hurried away.

Still staring at the reflection, Lori scratched her blond head. Why was Nora standing close by, watching, listening, waiting? Deciding to approach the old woman, Lori spun around.

The action startled Nora. In a panicked flurry she gathered her bags and scuttled away, slipping into the glass elevator just as the doors were closing.

You'd think I was the big bad wolf! Lori thought, shaking her head in confusion. If Miss Pringle was so frightened of people, why did she seem so interested in their conversations?

Checking her watch, Lori realized that this was one mystery she didn't have time to solve right now. She had to skedaddle downstairs and change into her uniform before the dinner crowd hit Tio's.

In a ranch house outside town, the atmosphere was hardly festive. The air was thick with tension and anger. No one spoke. No one looked at anyone else. Almost as soon as he walked in the door, Don escaped to the basement.

Straddling the seat of his editing bench, Don once again studied the return address on the fat envelope in his hand:
University of California—Los Angeles
School of Film Making and Production.

After wiping his sweaty palms on his jeans, Don ripped open the parchment envelope. His heart pounded as he unfolded the thick form.

APPLICATION MUST BE TYPED OR PRINTED
SUBMIT THREE COPIES

It was only a beginning. He needed a recommendation from George Colby, and he had to get accepted too. But at the moment Don felt as if he were holding the key to his future right in his own hands.

He'd been pretty gutsy, calling for the application. And he never would have tried if

Danielle hadn't spurred him on. Gorgeous, conniving Danielle.

He owed her. And he loved her.

The sound of heavy footsteps pounding down the stairs interrupted Don's train of thought. Quickly, he folded the application and shoved it back inside the envelope. His parents would never understand about his plans, his secret dreams.

"You've got some explaining to do," Mr. James growled, waving a piece of paper at Don. "The phone company is charging me for four calls to California. That's over twenty dollars!"

"I'll give you the money," Don told him.

"You're darn right you will! You know your mother and I have been scrimping and saving our pennies ever since I lost my job. We can't afford luxuries like long-distance calls."

Don shrugged. "I had a few calls to make, okay? I told you I'll pay you for them."

"Who do you know in California?" Mr. James asked, waving the bill through the air.

"No one."

"Then who did you call?"

With a frustrated sigh Don realized his father wouldn't stop hassling him until he gave him some answers. "If you've got to know, I was calling to get some information about a director out in Hollywood. And an application for a school that specializes in film making."

"Film making?" Mr. James snorted. "If I

had a dime for every film maker who's gone broke, I'd be a millionaire! Son, if I teach you just one lesson in life, it's value security. Go after a real profession and quit monkeying around with those home movies!"

Although Don could see that his father's temper was flaring, he couldn't back down now. "But, Dad, I like shooting film. Shouldn't I have a chance to work at something I enjoy?"

"By all means. But learn to enjoy a constructive profession—something that will pay the bills—instead of dreaming impossible dreams!"

Still clutching the bill, Mr. James's hand swept around in an arc, catching the edge of Don's camera. In one fast and furious second the camera flew off its tripod and landed on the linoleum floor with a resounding crash.

With clenched fists Don stared at the fallen camera. The lens was shattered. Even from where he stood, there was no mistaking the tiny shards of glass sparkling in a puddle on the basement floor.

"Is it broken?" Mr. James asked. "I—I'm sorry, son. But maybe it's an omen. It's time to buckle down and get serious about your life. Yes, I guess this is all for the best."

Don's dark eyes were unreadable as he stared at his father. How could his father be so insensitive? He'd just ruined Don's camera, and he actually seemed relieved.

The whole situation was hopeless. This man

didn't understand him. He was no father at all, not in the true sense of the word.

Silently, Don spun around and climbed the stairs, taking two steps in each long stride. He whipped past his mother in the kitchen, grabbed his jacket from the peg behind the door, and strode outside before anyone could stop him.

"Donald? Where do you think you're going?" she asked.

Hopping onto his bike, he fired up the engine and rolled down the driveway.

"Donald!" she called after him. "Get back here or you'll miss dinner!"

Good! he thought as he headed toward the back roads. *That'll be one less helping of misery for me.*

"Scram!" said Ernie Goldbloom. "Take a break and get out of here—while you can!"

"Thanks, Ernie." Lori pulled off her apron and stashed it under the counter. "I won't be long. Just want to get some air."

Actually, she wanted to check out a sale at D. B. Durant's. Forty percent off all fabric! Filled with excitement, Lori hurried along, dreaming of yards and yards of colorful, textured material for new designs.

Suddenly whipping around a corner, Lori stumbled to the floor and let out a yelp. In her rush she'd collided with another unsuspecting shopper!

"I'm so sorry . . ." she began, sitting up in the midst of the woman's scattered shopping bags. "I didn't mean to . . . Miss Pringle!"

Lori couldn't believe her eyes. After spending days searching for Nora, she'd actually run into her by accident!

Nora Pringle's beady eyes widened as she waved off Lori's apology. "It's quite all right," she murmured. Then she nervously dropped to her knees to collect the papers that had spilled forth from one torn shopping bag.

"Oh, let me help you with that." A sea of white surrounded Lori. Kneeling beside Nora, she started to help the woman gather and sort the papers.

Miss Pringle seemed edgy about accepting Lori's help. "I can do it, really—"

"But I insist," Lori interrupted, smoothing a stack of papers in her lap. "If I'd been looking where I was going, I wouldn't have bumped into . . ." Lori's voice trailed off as her eyes focused on the papers before her.

These weren't the scribbled notes of an eccentric old lady. They were computer print-outs!

FROM: Merivale Mall Corporation

TO: Ms. Nora Pringle, Shareholder

RE: Net Profits reported by FACADES, INC.

There were also reports on sales at the Shoe Hut, Platterpus . . . even Tio's!

Lori squinted, unable to believe what she

was reading. Why was Miss Pringle carrying around financial reports?

"Really," said a nervous Nora Pringle. "You don't have to waste your time with—"

"Hi, Lori!" Mike Sharp called.

Without looking up, Lori recognized the friendly voice of her uncle, the developer of Merivale Mall.

"Hello, Nora!" he added. Winking, he lowered his voice to say, "I see you're keeping right on top of the financial reports—as usual."

"Shhh!" Nora hissed. "Keep it down, Mike. And help me pick up this mess!"

Puzzled, Lori looked from her uncle to the bag lady. Obviously, they knew each other! But how?

"Uncle Mike," she said. "What's going on here?"

"Quiet!" Miss Pringle ordered, glancing around suspiciously.

"It's okay." Squatting down to help them, Mike Sharp picked up an armful of papers and stuffed them into one bag. "Let's just say that Nora and I are . . . associates."

"Michael"—Miss Pringle's voice was sharp with annoyance—"I think this conversation ought to take place in the privacy of your office—immediately!"

CHAPTER FOURTEEN

"Coffee, Nora?" Danielle's father asked.

"Yes, please. Cream, no sugar." Sitting with her back straight and her legs crossed, Nora Pringle looked positively regal in the plush surroundings of Mike Sharp's office. Although she still wore the raggedy clothes, she had removed her purple beret to fluff up her curly gray hair.

"Coffee, Lori?"

"No, thanks, Uncle Mike." Lori was too overwhelmed to consider anything but the strange woman before her.

"I can tell you're burning with curiosity, young lady," Miss Pringle said. "First off, I must ask you not to reveal my true identity to anyone else." Her dark eyes earnest, she repeated, "Please do not . . . blow my cover!"

138

Still too shocked to speak, Lori merely nodded.

Mike Sharp handed Nora a cup of coffee, then sat down in the enormous leather chair behind his desk. "You might say that Nora is a key personality in the operation of Merivale Mall. She's always been a staunch supporter, and, to date, she's still the principal shareholder."

Nora Pringle—financial maven! Lori's blue eyes were clouded with confusion. That meant Nora was a wealthy woman! "Then why do you go around dressed like a bag lady? Muttering and scribbling and rooting through those shopping bags?"

"I've been carefully observing each store, studying traffic patterns, making notes for improvements." Once wary and glazed, Nora's dark eyes glowed with enthusiasm as she spoke about marketing and high finance.

"You see," she continued, "our corporation receives a percentage of each shop's profits. So, naturally, I'm extremely interested in suggesting ways to increase sales."

Lori shrugged. "That part makes sense to me. But why the secrecy—and the tattered clothes?"

"I don't want the shop owners to know who I am or what I'm up to. Otherwise, they may try to influence my decision or manipulate sales." Miss Pringle picked up her beret, fingering the thin lining. "This disguise insures an objective survey. And the shopping bags are perfect! They allow me to carry around financial reports, so all the information I need is right at my fingertips!"

As the pieces of the puzzle fell into place, a humongous blush stung Lori's face. She was a first-class fool!

"Pretty crafty of Nora, don't you think?" asked Danielle's father.

"Very crafty," Lori agreed. *So crafty, you completely duped me!* "You must have thought I was nuts, chasing you around with food and clothes." A thoughtful frown shadowed her pretty face. "Imagine, treating the richest woman in Merivale like a charity case!"

Nora smiled. "Actually, I found your concern rather touching. And I especially liked the way you stood up to those nasty boys. You have spunk, young lady. I admire that in a person."

"And that comes from the woman who invented the word!" Mike Sharp added with a chuckle.

"Furthermore, I was planning to speak with you—even before our little collision." She leaned forward, completely capturing Lori's attention. "I've been keeping an eye on you. Those clothes you make are causing quite a stir among teens in this mall."

"Thanks," Lori said. "It's just a hobby, but I have a lot of fun with it."

"Is that so?" Miss Pringle uncrossed her legs and smoothed her raggedy skirt. "Well, maybe it's time to cash in on that fun. How would you like to go into business?"

Stunned, Lori didn't know what to say.

"If you design and produce a line of outfits like that snappy number you were wearing earlier, I'll agree to be your principal backer. That means I'll pay your expenses and arrange to feature the clothes at a shop in the mall."

Nora turned to Danielle's father. "What do you think, Mike? Perhaps Snazzz! Or maybe Facades."

Facades! My very own designs! Creations by Lori Randall. . . Glorious possibilities exploded in Lori's mind. All her wildest dreams were coming true!

"I think Facades just might be interested," Mike Sharp agreed.

Lori's pulse was racing, making it difficult to think rationally. "It sounds wonderful," she said, trying to keep her feet on the ground, her head out of the clouds.

She would have to work like crazy, maybe even cut down on her social life. But Patsy and Ann were such supportive friends. And Nick— handsome, good-natured Nick—would understand. He always encouraged Lori to go after her dreams.

"I'll have to ask my parents, of course."

"Of course," Nora agreed. "But I think

they'll agree this is an excellent opportunity for you. Talk to them, then come see me. We'll start you off with a small advance of . . . oh, let's say, a thousand dollars."

Lori's jaw dropped at the mention of such an outrageous sum. A thousand dollars would buy out half the fabric at D. B. Durant's! Now she *knew* she was dreaming!

"That's . . . that's very generous," Lori said breathlessly.

"Generous?" Nora's dark eyes were skeptical. "No, dear, it's merely a solid investment."

Overwhelmed, Lori turned to her uncle.

"Sounds like a sweet deal to me," he said. "If I were you, I'd consider taking Nora up on her offer." He patted the arms of his big leather chair. "Nora and I made a deal years ago— and I don't have a single regret!"

"Think about it," Nora said.

Mike Sharp's cheerful smile was encouraging as he whispered to Lori, "This is an opportunity you shouldn't miss!"

CHAPTER FIFTEEN

A star flared for a moment, then shot across the black sky, leaving a brief thread of light in its path.

That's me—a shooting star. From his bed of pine needles, Don lay on his back staring at the vast, open sky, wishing he were anywhere on earth but Merivale.

Shoot out of here—and never come back. Was the star a sign? His old man's message had been clear enough. Mr. and Mrs. James certainly wouldn't miss their youngest son. So what was keeping him here?

Danielle.

He loved her. He wanted to be with her. He definitely didn't want to leave her behind, but he was dying a slow death, living under his parents' roof. He had to get out.

Sometimes I'm tempted to ride off . . . he'd told her.

She'd laughed, then said, *But you'd have to take me with you*.

Rolling to his feet, Don scanned the empty field. Would Danielle go away with him?

But even as he asked himself the question, Don knew it was impossible. Danielle belonged here. He had nothing, but she had friends, a home—a life. And he couldn't take her away from all that. It would be wrong—unfair to her.

Don jumped on his bike. A moment later the engine roared to life. He tore out of the field, leaving a cloud of dust in his wake.

It was late. His parents would be in bed by now. He could slip in and out of the house before they lost a wink of precious sleep.

And then the only thing that would stand between him and the open road was one beautiful, smart girl with red hair and emerald eyes, sultry eyes that a guy could get lost in.

It started as a soft rustle, like the sound the tree branches made when the wind pushed them against the window.

Lost in thought, Danielle barely noticed the sound as she hugged her pillow.

Then it happened again.

It must be raining, she thought, still caught up in her worries. For the first time since their magic week of romance, Don had let a night pass without calling her. Even worse, when she'd phoned his house Mrs. James had told her that he'd disappeared.

Where in the world was Don?

When her window rattled a third time, Danielle jumped off the edge of her bed. What *was* that?

Standing by the window, she saw Don's old T-bird parked in the driveway below. He was leaning against the car, pitching gravel at her bedroom window.

"Stop!" She laughed, waving at him. *So . . . he's come to make amends*, she thought, pulling on a satin robe and belting it at the waist.

I'll forgive him this time—only because I love him. Giddy with relief, Danielle raced down the stairs, hardly caring about her disheveled hair and lack of make-up.

She ran out the front door and threw herself in his arms.

"Wow!" Don lifted her off her feet in a powerful hug. "I should have thrown rocks at your window sooner!"

As he lowered her to her feet, Danielle's lips curved in a pout. "I still haven't completely forgiven you for not calling. What happened to you tonight?"

Don raked his fingers through his hair, his dark eyes haunted and troubled. A moment later the trunk of his T-bird caught Danielle's eye. It was gaping open, the lid roped down over . . . over a stack of boxes!

Danielle's heart thudded in her chest. "What's going on?" When he didn't answer immediately, she stepped toward the car and peered in the window. Camera equipment and boxes covered the back seat and floor.

"I'm leaving, Red. Heading out to California."

Leaving! Danielle spun around to face him, then nearly collapsed against the car. Everything had been going perfectly! How could he leave now?

"I haven't heard from George Colby yet, but that doesn't matter. When I get to L.A. I'll send him my new address. I've got to get away tonight."

"Why?" Danielle's voice was a hoarse croak. "Has something horrible happened?"

Shoving his hands into his pockets, Don shrugged. "It's my parents. My father and I had it out. He ended up smashing my camera and telling me to look for a more solid profession." Don's laugh was laced with pain. "Can you believe that? Fatherly advice, from one loser to another."

Although Danielle understood why Don was upset, a fight with his father was hardly reason to leave Merivale—and her—behind! "Your father's a fool, Don. But you're very talented." She reached forward and touched the leather sleeve of his jacket. "Don't worry. It'll all blow over. Come tomorrow morning, he won't even remember—"

"I'll be gone by tomorrow," Don interrupted. "Don't you see, Red? If I stay here, I'll end up just like them. Unhappy. Struggling. Wondering what would have happened if I took a chance. Sometimes you just have to shoot the moon and go for it. I have to leave now . . . or never."

He stepped forward, tenderly placing his hands on her shoulders. "Tonight I'm going to ditch Merivale and take to the highway."

Danielle's breath caught in her throat. She couldn't believe this was happening to her! But the dark gleam in Don's eyes told her that he was dead serious. Her shaking hands gripped his sleeve, clinging to him as the world rocked around her.

The night sounds of chirruping crickets filled the air, closing in around them. Danielle's heart was pounding so hard, she was sure Don could hear it too.

"What about high school?" she asked, finally gaining control of her voice. "I mean, how will you finish? You'll have to get a degree before U.C.L.A. will let you in."

"I don't know." Don's hands slid down her arms, sending shivers through her. "I haven't figured everything out yet, but I'm going to make it work."

He cupped her smooth hands and held them against his chest. "I'm going to chase this dream, no matter what. You showed me how important it is to reach for the stars."

Me? Danielle was stunned. When did she do that? She swallowed. A tight knot was forming in her throat. She couldn't let Don go! Not when they were so much in love.

"Take me with you," she pleaded, her heartbeat racing. "Don"—her voice wavered—"I love you, really and truly. I don't want to stay in Merivale without you!"

Yes, that was it! Danielle's eyes began to sparkle as she pictured their escape. It would be wildly romantic—they'd be the rage of Merivale for years! Not to mention the prospect of life in Hollywood with Don. The sunny coast of California . . . movie stars . . . fancy cars. And she would never have to hear her parents arguing again. The plan was almost like a fantastic movie. Could they ride off into the sunset together?

But a little voice inside brought her back to earth. Danielle couldn't imagine leaving Merivale forever. How would she finish high school? What about her friends . . . and her family? Deep down inside she knew she would miss them.

The night air was chilly, but Danielle's hands were warm, cocooned in Don's palms. Tears stung her eyes as she stared at him, hoping, wondering if love could make a difference for them. Didn't love make everything perfect?

"I love you too, Red. And I'd love to take you with me." He paused and took a deep breath. "But I can't. You've got a decent life here. I know your parents have their problems, but they do care about you. I can't steal you away from them. At least, not yet."

Danielle's knees began to tremble. So Don was going it alone. Although she wanted to fight him, she knew it was the right decision for both of them. Don was right, but the reality of the situation cut her. How could she say good-bye to the only boy she'd ever loved?

"Promise me one thing," Don whispered, squeezing her hands. "Always remember that I love you."

"Always," she murmured, her throat tight with emotion.

He smiled crookedly. "I guess this is good-bye, Red."

"No! We'll never say good-bye. We'll be together again—someday. Won't we?" she asked hoarsely.

"Sure, Red. Someday."

Suddenly Danielle couldn't hold back the tears. They pooled in her emerald eyes and spilled down her cheeks. This couldn't be happening to her! She couldn't be losing the only boy she'd ever loved, the only person she'd ever shared her hopes and dreams with!

But she was.

Gently, Don wiped a teardrop from her cheek. "Take it easy, Red." He kissed her lightly on the lips, then turned and slid into his car. He rolled down the window for one last, lingering look. "Guess I'll have to ride off into the sunset alone."

A moment later he was pulling away, gravel crunching under the tires of his car.

"Please . . . please don't go," Danielle called out in the darkness. Sobbing, she watched as the red taillights shrank to tiny red dots—then vanished into the night. He was gone. In one short night her whole life had collapsed.

A fresh wave of tears struck. She rubbed her eyes, then ran inside, wishing this whole scene were just a nightmare that would flee the minute she woke up.

Huddled in the corner of her bed, she wondered what she would do without Don. Oh, lots of guys at Atwood would jump at the chance to date Danielle Sharp. She could have her pick of any guy in Merivale—handsome hunks with money, sporty cars, and slick clothes.

Tomorrow she could piant the seeds for a new romance.

But tonight . . . She shivered. Tonight she

was still in love with Don James. She wanted him to hold her, to tenderly brush away the tears from her cheeks as he'd done before. What a mess. For once in her life Danielle Sharp wanted something that she couldn't have.

Don was gone, riding west, off to a new life. Don was gone . . . forever.

And she would miss him so much.